MW01287514

The Seven Deadly Sins

by Thornton Wilder

ISBN 978-0-573-70004-0   Printed in U.S.A.   #28073

MUSIC USE NOTE

Licensees are solely responsible for obtaining formal written permission from copyright owners to use copyrighted music in the performance of this play and are strongly cautioned to do so. If no such permission is obtained by the licensee, then the licensee must use only original music that the licensee owns and controls. Licensees are solely responsible and liable for all music clearances and shall indemnify the copyright owners of the play and their licensing agent, Samuel French, Inc., against any costs, expenses, losses and liabilities arising from the use of music by licensees.

IMPORTANT BILLING AND CREDIT REQUIREMENTS

All producers of *THE SEVEN DEADLY SINS must* give credit to the Author of the Play in all programs distributed in connection with performances of the Play, and in all instances in which the title of the Play appears for the purposes of advertising, publicizing or otherwise exploiting the Play and/or a production. The name of the Author *must* appear on a separate line on which no other name appears, immediately following the title and *must* appear in size of type not less than fifty percent of the size of the title type.

All producers of *A RINGING OF DOORBELLS* and *IN SHAKESPEARE AND THE BIBLE* must print the following credit 1/3 of the size of the author's name in the same boldness of type on the initial credits page of all programs distributed in connection with performances of the Play: "This/these [or title of play if more appropriate] became available through the research and editing of F.J."

FOREWORD TO *THE SINS* AND *AGES*

Welcome to a new collection of Thornton Wilder's last plays—a series of one acts that were part of his extravagantly ambitious project to create two seven-play cycles based on the deadly sins and the ages of man. From the time he began dreaming up plays as a boy, Wilder's vision of the theater transcended conventional boundaries, and up to the end of his life his vision continually evolved and expanded, as these plays demonstrate.

In 1956, Wilder began working on what would prove to be his final dramatic works, seeking not only to explore the theatrical possibilities inherent in the sins and ages, but (as he phrased it in his private journal on Christmas Day, 1960) to "offer each play in the series as representing, also, a different mode of playwriting: Grand Guignol, Chekhov, Noh play, etc., etc." In short, he envisioned nothing less than a *tour de force* of dramatic theme and form encapsulated in the economy and intensity of the one act play.

Wilder did not complete the challenge he set for himself, but he came close. The surviving work enriches his dramatic legacy and deserves to be remembered as more than a footnote to his lifelong conviction (written soon after *Our Town* opened on Broadway in 1938): "The theater offers to imaginative narration its highest possibilities."

The *Sins* and *Ages* Then and Now

A brief overview of the history of these plays will help readers "place" them in Wilder's career as a dramatist. Two *Sins* (*Pride* and *Sloth*) premiered in English at a special event in Berlin in 1957 (with Wilder performing in *Pride*). For reasons that have never been clear, for he enjoyed the experience and felt that plays did well, he withdrew them from the event. That same year a third *Sin* (*Gluttony*), written as the satyr play for Wilder's full length drama, *The Alcestiad*, proved successful in its premiere on the stage of Zurich's fabled Schauspielhaus.

Five years passed before the continuation of his ambitious scheme appeared on a stage in the United States. In January 1962, two new *Ages* (*Infancy* and *Childhood*) and a new *Sin* (*Lust*) opened at Circle in the Square, then located Off Broadway on Bleecker Street, to the reported largest pre-opening advanced sale in that stage's then 11-year history. Billed as "Plays for Bleecker Street," the show ran for 349 performances.

Then silence. After "Plays for Bleecker Street" closed, no more *Sins* or *Ages* appeared. When Thornton Wilder died in 1975 the public record of his ambitious fourteen plays scheme contained only four plays— two *Ages* (*Infancy* and *Childhood*) and two *Sins* (*Lust* and *Gluttony*).

Today, as evidenced by the content of this volume, eleven of Wilder's *Sins* and *Ages* are available for production: a completed cycle of the seven deadly sins and four of the seven ages of man.[1] The source of the seven "new" plays is no secret. The missing pieces were found in Thornton Wilder's archives at Yale. From this source, starting in 1995, his literary executor and family released the two plays withdrawn in 1957, a completed *Avarice*, and four additional titles (*Youth*, *The Rivers Under the Earth* [*Middle Age*][2], *Envy* and *Wrath*) recovered by the actor, director and close friend of Wilder's, F.J. O'Neil. (Mr. O'Neil's valuable notes on the origin of each of these missing links follow the text of each play.)

The public reception of Thornton Wilder's long lost and new plays was gratifying. *Sloth* was selected as one of the Best American Short Plays of 1994-95. In 1997, the Centenary of the playwright's birth, Kevin Kline starred in a premiere reading in New York of *Avarice*, and the works recovered by Mr. O'Neil served as the center pieces of Actors Theatre of Louisville's 13th Annual Brown-Forman Classics in Context Festival. Finally, as the capstone to the Centenary celebration, TCG Press in 1997 published the eleven *Sins* and *Ages* in Volume I of *The Collected Short Plays of Thornton Wilder*.

Wilder never followed conventional theatrical practice. As a young writer in his *Classic One Act Plays* of 1931, he swept away scenery and played provocative games with time and place. In these *Sins* and *Ages*, his farewell as a playwright, he is no less adventurous by way of settings, techniques, stage-craft and themes. One artistic trend of the day especially "fired his imagination" where these plays are concerned: his passionate belief in the value of the arena stage. "The boxed set play," he wrote in 1961, "encourages the anecdote...The unencumbered stage encourages the truth in everyone." Wilder felt so strongly that audiences should be seated as close to the actors as possible that Samuel French, for several years, was only permitted to license these plays to companies agreeing to perform them on a three-sided thrust or arena stage.

* * *

As part of its celebration of Wilder's one act plays, Samuel French and the Wilder family take great pleasure in issuing new acting editions for the *Sins* and *Ages* that were long in print and, for the first time, acting editions for the seven "new" Wilder works. We invite those performing or teaching these plays to visit www.thorntonwilder.com for additional information.

Tappan Wilder
Literary Executor for Thornton Wilder

---

1 No additional one acts remain to be discovered in Thornton Wilder's archives at Yale.
2 We believe that Wilder intended *Rivers Under the Earth* to represent middle age.

CONTENTS

ONE

THE DRUNKEN SISTERS

(Gluttony)

CHARACTERS

CLOTHO　⎤
LACHESIS　⎬ — The Three Fates
ATROPOS　⎦

APOLLO

SETTING

The time of Admetus, King of Thessaly.

EDITOR'S NOTE

A pronunciation guide for key terms in this play is available on www.ThorntonWilder.com.

*(The only objects necessary for the setting of this play are a platform about two feet high on which the **THREE FATES** are seated, and the bench beneath them. The bench is largely hidden by their voluminous draperies. They wear the masks of old women, touched by the grotesque but with vestiges of nobility. Seated from the players' Right to Left are **CLOTHO** with her spindle, **LACHESIS** with the bulk of the thread of life on her lap, and **ATROPOS** with her scissors. The designer should resort to every device in order to make them appear enormous and of wide knee-span. They rock back and forth as they work, passing the threads from right to left. The audience watches them for a time in silence, broken only by a faint humming from* **CLOTHO.***)*

CLOTHO. What is it that goes first on four legs, then on two legs? Don't tell me! Don't tell me!

LACHESIS. *(bored)* You know it!

CLOTHO. Let me pretend that I don't know it.

ATROPOS. There are no new riddles. We know them all.

LACHESIS. How boring our life is without riddles! Clotho, make up a riddle.

CLOTHO. Be quiet, then, and give me a moment to think… What is it that… What is it that…?

(Enter **APOLLO,** *disguised. He wears a cone-shaped straw hat with a wide brim to conceal his face. Three flagons are hanging from a rope around his neck.)*

APOLLO. *(to the audience)* I am Apollo. In the disguise of a kitchen boy. I hate disguises. And I hate drunkenness – but see these bottles I have hanging around my neck? I hate lies and stratagems; but I've come here to do crookedly what even Allfather Zeus could not do without guile. These are the great sisters – the

Fates. Clotho weaves the threads of life; Lachesis measures the length of each; Atropos cuts them short. I have come to do a thing which has never been done before – to extend human life; to arrest the scissors of Atropos. Oh, to change the order of the universe.

ATROPOS. Sister! Your elbow! Do your work without striking me.

LACHESIS. I can't help it – this thread is s-o-o l-o-o-ong! Never have I had to reach so far.

CLOTHO. Long and gray and dirty! All those years a slave!

LACHESIS. So it is! *(to* **ATROPOS***)* Cut it, dear sister. *(***ATROPOS** *cuts it – click!)* And now this one; cut this. It's a blue one – blue for bravery, blue and short.

ATROPOS. So easy to see!

(click)

LACHESIS. You almost cut that purple one, Atropos.

ATROPOS. This one? Purple for a king?

LACHESIS. Yes; watch what you're doing, dear. It's the life of Admetus, King of Thessaly.

APOLLO. *(aside)* Aie!

LACHESIS. I've marked it clearly. He's to die at sunset.

APOLLO. *(to the audience)* No! No!

LACHESIS. He's the favorite of Apollo, as was his father before him, and all that tiresome house of Thessaly. The queen Alcestis will be a widow tonight.

APOLLO. *(to the audience)* Alcestis! Alcestis! No!

LACHESIS. There'll be howling in Thessaly. There'll be rolling on the ground and tearing of garments…Not now dear; there's an hour yet.

APOLLO. *(aside)* To work! To work, Apollo the Crooked! *(He starts the motions of running furiously while remaining in one place, but stops suddenly and addresses the audience.)* Is there anyone here who does not know that old story – the reason why King Admetus and his queen Alcestis are dear to me? *(He sits on the ground and continues talking with raised forefinger.)* Was it ten years ago? I am little concerned with time. I am the god of the sun; it is always light where I am. Perhaps ten years ago. My father and the father of us all was filled up with anger against me. What had I done? *(He moves his finger back and forth.)* Do not ask that now; let it be forgotten…He laid upon me a punishment. He ordered that I should descend to earth and live for a year among men – *I*, as a man among men, as a servant. Half hidden, known and not known, I chose to be a herdsman of King Admetus of Thessaly. I lived the life of a man, as close to them as I am to you now, as close to the just and to the unjust. Each day the King gave orders to the other herdsmen and myself; each day the Queen gave thought to what went well or ill with us and our families. I came to love King Admetus and Queen Alcestis and through them I came to love all men. And now Admetus must die. *(rising)* No! I have laid my plans. I shall prevent it. To work. To work, Apollo the Crooked. *(He again starts the motions of running furiously while remaining in one place. He complains noisily.)* Oh, my back! Aie, aie. They beat me, but worst of all they've made me late. I'll be beaten again.

LACHESIS. Who's the sniveler?

APOLLO. Don't stop me now. I haven't a moment to talk. I'm late already. Besides, my errand's a terrible secret. I can't say a word.

ATROPOS. Throw your yarn around him, Lachesis. What's the fool doing with a secret? It's we who have all the secrets.

*(The threads in the laps of the Sisters are invisible to the audience. **LACHESIS** now rises and swings her hands three times in wide circles above her head as though she were about to fling a lasso, then hurls the noose across the stage. **APOLLO** makes the gesture of being caught. With each strong pull by **LACHESIS**, **APOLLO** is dragged nearer to her. During the following speeches **LACHESIS** lifts her end of the strands high in the air, alternately pulling **APOLLO** up, almost strangling him, and flinging him again to the ground.)*

APOLLO. Ladies, beautiful ladies, let me go. If I'm late all Olympus will be in an uproar. Aphrodite will be mad with fear – but oh, already I've said too much. My orders were to come immediately, and to say nothing especially not to women. The thing's of no interest to men. Dear ladies, let me go.

ATROPOS. Pull on your yarn, sister.

APOLLO. You're choking me. You're squeezing me to death.

LACHESIS. *(forcefully)* Stop your whining and tell your secret at once.

APOLLO. I can't. I dare not.

ATROPOS. Pull harder, sister. Boy, speak or strangle.

(She makes the gesture of choking him.)

APOLLO. Ow! Ow! – Wait! I'll tell the half of it, if you let me go.

ATROPOS. Tell the whole or we'll hang you up in the air in that noose.

APOLLO. I'll tell, I'll tell. But – *(He looks about him fearfully.)* – promise me! Swear by the Styx that you'll not tell anyone, and swear by Lethe that you'll forget it.

LACHESIS. We have only one oath – by Acheron. And we never swear it – least of all to a sniveling slave. Tell us what you know, or you'll be by all three rivers in a minute.

APOLLO. I tremble at what I am about to say. I...ssh...I carry...here...in these bottles...Oh, ladies, let me go. Let me go.

CLOTHO & ATROPOS. Pull, sister.

APOLLO. No! No! I'll tell you. I am carrying the wine for... for Aphrodite. Once every ten days she renews her beauty...by...drinking this.

ATROPOS. Liar! Fool! She has nectar and ambrosia, as they all have.

APOLLO. *(confidentially)* But is she not the fairest?... It is the love gift of Hephaistos; from the vineyards of Dionysos; from grapes ripened under the eye of Apollo – of Apollo who tells no lies.

SISTERS. *(confidentially to one another in blissful anticipation)* Sisters!

ATROPOS. *(like sugar)* Pass the bottles up, dear boy.

APOLLO. *(in terror)* Not that! Ladies! It is enough that I have told you the secret! Not that!

ATROPOS. Surely, Lachesis, you can find on your lap the thread of this worthless slave – a yellow one destined for a long life?

APOLLO. *(falling on his knees)* Spare me!

ATROPOS. *(to LACHESIS)* Look, that's it – the sallow one, with the tangle in it of dishonesty, and the stiffness of obstinacy, and the ravel – ravel of stupidity. Pass it over to me, dear.

APOLLO. *(his forehead touching the floor)* Oh, that I had never been born!

LACHESIS. *(to ATROPOS)* This is it. *(with a sigh)* I'd planned to give him five score.

APOLLO. *(rising and extending the bottles, sobbing)* Here, take them! I'll be killed anyway. Aphrodite will kill me. My life's over.

ATROPOS. *(strongly, as the SISTERS take the bottles)* Not one more word out of you. Put your hand on your mouth. We're tired of listening to you.

(APOLLO, released of the noose, flings himself facedown upon the ground, his shoulders heaving. The SISTERS put the flagons to their lips. They drink and moan with pleasure.)

LACHESIS. Sisters!

ATROPOS. Sisters!

CLOTHO. Sisters!

LACHESIS. Sister, how do I look?

ATROPOS. Oh, I could eat you. And I?

CLOTHO. Sister, how do I look?

LACHESIS. Beautiful! Beautiful! And I?

ATROPOS. And not a mirror on all the mountain, or a bit of still water, to tell us which of us is the fairest.

LACHESIS. *(dreamily, passing her hand over her face)* I feel like…I feel as I did when Kronos followed me about, trying to catch me in a dark corner.

ATROPOS. Poseidon was beside himself – dashing across the plains trying to engulf me.

CLOTHO. My own father – who can blame him? – began to forget himself.

ATROPOS. *(whispering)* This is not such a worthless fellow, after all. And he's not bad-looking. *(to* CLOTHO*)* Ask him what he sees.

LACHESIS. Ask him which of us is the fairest.

CLOTHO. Boy! Boy! You bay meek. I mean, you…you may thpeak. Thpeak to him, Lakethith; I've lotht my tongue.

LACHESIS. Boy, look at us well! You may tell us which is the fairest.

(Each of the SISTERS *is drunk in a different way.* CLOTHO *becomes a little girl.* LACHESIS *arrogant and quarrelsome,* ATROPOS *tearful.)*

CLOTHO. Of courth, I'm the yougeth. I've always been a darling. Everybody saith–simply everybody saith– Darling Clotho. Thweet Clotho.

LACHESIS. *(striking her)* Yes, youngest and silliest– and vulgarest. I don't care who the fool says is fairest. I wouldn't expect to find taste in a kitchen boy. Who cares for the admiration of the marketplace?

ATROPOS. No one has ever been just to me. People say that I'm cruel. I'm not cruel. I've the tenderest heart in the world. I spend my life doing my duty, and what do I get for it? —ingratitude!

(They start talking simultaneously. LACHESIS *is the loudest.)*

LACHESIS. Go find a judge who knows beauty when he sees it. Not a shallow pettiness, like you, Clotho, nor a bitter face like yours, Atropos, but soul. Soul. Spirit. Majesty. Dignity. Soul.

CLOTHO. Of courth, I'm *little*. I've always been little. When I path'd everybody said: mi-mi-mi-mi; come here, you little darling. Mi-mi-mi-mi, you little darling.

ATROPOS. Hidden away on this mountain. One injustice after another. And what do I get for it? —ingratitude. the tenderest heart in the world—that's what I have.

LACHESIS. (*silencing them*) Hold your tongues, geese, and let's put the question to the young man. Boy, get up. Don't be afraid. Tell us: in your opinion, which of us is the fairest?

(**APOLLO** *has remained face downward on the ground. He now rises and gazes at the* **SISTERS**. *He acts as if blinded he cowers and uncovers his eyes, gazing first at one and then at another.*)

APOLLO. What have I done? This splendor! What have I done? You – and you – and you! Kill me if you will, but I cannot say which one is the fairest. (*falling on his knees*) Oh, ladies – if so much beauty has not made you cruel, let me now go and hide myself. Aphrodite will hear of this. Let me escape to Crete and take up my old work.

ATROPOS. What was your former work, dear boy?

APOLLO. I helped my father in the marketplace; I was a teller of stories and riddles.

(*The* **SISTERS** *are transfixed. Then almost with a scream.*)

SISTERS. What's that? What's that you said?

APOLLO. A teller of stories and riddles. Do the beautiful ladies enjoy riddles?

SISTERS. (*rocking from side to side and slapping one another*) Sisters, do we enjoy riddles?

ATROPOS. Oh, he would only know the *old* ones. Puh! The blind horse...the big toe...

LACHESIS. The cloud...the eyelashes of Hera...

CLOTHO. (*harping on one string*) What is it that first goes on four legs...?

ATROPOS. The porpoise…Etna…

APOLLO. Everyone knows those! I have some new ones –

SISTERS. *(again, a scream)* New ones!

APOLLO. *(slowly)* What is it that is necessary to –

   (He pauses. The **SISTERS** *are riveted.)*

LACHESIS. Go on, boy, go on. What is it that is necessary to –

APOLLO. But – I only play for forfeits. See! If I lose…

CLOTHO. If you looth, you mutht tell uth which one ith the faireth.

APOLLO. No! No! I dare not!

LACHESIS. *(sharply)* Yes!

APOLLO. And if I win?

ATROPOS. Win? Idiot! Stupid! Slave! No one has ever won from us.

APOLLO. But if I win?

LACHESIS. He doesn't know who we are!

APOLLO. But if I win?

CLOTHO. The fool talkth of winning!

APOLLO. If I win, you must grant me one wish. One wish, any wish.

LACHESIS. Yes, yes. Oh, what a tedious fellow! Go on with your riddle. What is it that is necessary to –

APOLLO. Swear by Acheron!

CLOTHO & LACHESIS. We swear! By Acheron! By Acheron!

APOLLO. *(to* **ATROPOS***)* You, too.

ATROPOS. *(after a moment's brooding resistance, loudly)* By Acheron!

APOLLO. Then: ready?

LACHESIS. Wait! One moment. *(leaning toward* **ATROPOS**, *confidentially)* The sun is near setting. Do not forget the thread of Ad – You know, the thread of Ad –

ATROPOS. What? What Ad? What are you whispering about, silly?

LACHESIS. *(somewhat louder)* Not to forget the thread of Admetus, King of Thessaly. At sundown. Have you lost your shears, Atropos?

ATROPOS. Oh, stop your buzzing and fussing and tend to your own business. Of course I haven't lost my shears. Go on with your riddle, boy!

APOLLO. So! I'll give you as much time as it takes to recite the names of the Muses and their mother.

LACHESIS. Hm! Nine and one. Well, begin!

APOLLO. What is it that is necessary to every life – and that can save only one?

(The **SISTERS** *rock back and forth with closed eyes, mumbling the words of the riddle. Suddenly* **APOLLO** *starts singing his invocation to the Muses.)*

Mnemosyne, mother of the nine;
Polyhymnia, incense of the gods –

LACHESIS. *(shrieks)* Don't sing! Unfair! How can we think?

CLOTHO. Stop your ears, sister.

ATROPOS. Unfair! *(murmuring)* What is it that can save every life –

(They put their fingers in their ears.)

APOLLO. Erato, voice of love;
Euterpe, help me now.
Calliope, thief of our souls;
Urania, clothed of the stars;
Clio of the backward glances;
Euterpe, help me now.
Terpsichore of the beautiful ankles;
Thalia of long laughter;
Melpomene, dreaded and welcome;
Euterpe, help me now.

(then in a loud voice) Forfeit! Forfeit!

*(***CLOTHO** *and* **ATROPOS** *bury their faces in* **LACHESIS***'s neck, moaning.)*

LACHESIS. *(in a dying voice)* What is the answer?

APOLLO. *(flinging away his hat, triumphantly)* Myself! Apollo the sun.

SISTERS. Apollo! You?

LACHESIS. *(savagely)* Pah! What life can you save?

APOLLO. My forfeit! One wish! One life! That life of Admetus, King of Thessaly.

(A horrified clamor arises from the SISTERS.)

SISTERS. Fraud! Impossible! Not to be thought of!

APOLLO. By Acheron.

SISTERS. Against all law. Zeus will judge. Fraud.

APOLLO. *(warning)* By Acheron.

SISTERS. Zeus! We will go to Zeus about it. He will decide.

APOLLO. Zeus swears by Acheron and keeps his oath. *(sudden silence)*

ATROPOS. *(decisive but ominous)* You will have your wish – the life of King Admetus. But –

APOLLO. *(triumphantly)* I shall have the life of Admetus!

SISTERS. But –

APOLLO. I shall have the life of Admetus! What is your but?

ATROPOS. Someone else must die in his stead.

APOLLO. *(lightly)* Oh – choose some slave. Some gray and greasy thread on your lap, divine Lachesis.

LACHESIS. *(outraged)* What? You ask me to take a life?

ATROPOS. You ask us to murder?

CLOTHO. Apollo thinks that we are criminals?

APOLLO. *(beginning to be fearful)* Then, great sisters, how is this to be done?

LACHESIS. Me – an assassin? *(she spreads her arms wide and says solemnly)* Over my left hand is Chance; over my right hand is Necessity.

APOLLO. Then, gracious sisters, how will this be done?

LACHESIS. Someone must *give* his life for Admetus – of free choice and will. Over such deaths we have no control. Neither Chance nor Necessity rules the free offering of the will. Someone must choose to die in the place of Admetus, King of Thessaly.

APOLLO. *(covering his face with his hands)* No! No! I see it all! *(with a loud cry)* Alcestis! Alcestis! *(And he runs stumbling from the scene.)*

End of Play

TWO

BERNICE

(Pride)

CHARACTERS

MR. MALLISON, Mr. Walbeck's lawyer, fifty-nine
BERNICE MAYHEW, Mr. Walbeck's maid, fifty
THE DRIVER
MR. WALBECK, forty-seven

SETTING

Drawing room of a house in Chicago, 1911.

(Door into the hall at the back. All we need see are an elaborate, but not weighty, table in the center and two chairs. At the front of the stage are some andirons and a poker, indicating a fireplace. **MALLISON**, *fifty-nine, all a lawyer, now very nervous, is standing before the table holding an open watch in his hand. By the door is* **BERNICE**, *colored, fifty, in a maid's uniform.)*

MALLISON. Remind me…remind me, please…your name?

BERNICE. *(unimpressed)* Bernice.

MALLISON. Thank you. – Now Mr. Burgess, your employer, may be a little bit…moody. You do whatever he wants. Have you enough help to run the house?

BERNICE. I did what you told me. There's Jason for the heavy work and the furnace. This Mr. Burgess – will he be alone in this house?

MALLISON. Alone? Oh! Most probably. At all events, you are in charge. Get whatever help you need. I am Mr. Burgess's lawyer, but he will be getting another lawyer soon. All your bills will be paid, I'm sure…You have some dinner waiting for him now?

BERNICE. *(slowly)* Why do you talk so funny about this Mr. Burgess? Is he coming from the crazy house or something?

MALLISON. *(outraged)* No, indeed!! I don't know where you got such an idea. All that's expected of you is…uh… good meals and a well-run house.

BERNICE. You talk very funny, Mr. Mallison.

MALLISON. *(after swallowing with dignity and glaring at her)* Mrs. Willard recommended you as an experienced cook and housekeeper, Bernice. My duty ends there.

BERNICE. I don't have to take any jobs unless I likes them, Mr. Mallison. I never agrees to work any place more than three days. Mrs. Willard don't like it, but that's my terms – if I likes it, I stays.

MALLISON. Well, I hope you like it here. You're getting very well paid and you can ask for any further help you need – within reason. There's an automobile stopping before the door now. I think you'd better go to the door.

*(**BERNICE** doesn't move. Arms akimbo she looks musingly at **MALLISON**.)*

BERNICE. I seen people like you before…You're up to something.

(The front door bell rings.)

MALLISON. I don't like your tone. You've been engaged to work here – for three days, anyway. You can begin by answering that door bell.

*(**BERNICE** goes out. **MALLISON** straightens his clothes, goes to the table and picks up his briefcase, then stands waiting with pursed lips. Sounds of altercation from the hall.)*

DRIVER'S VOICE. All right! The price is twenty dollars. But if I'd know'd it was a night like this –

*(Enter the **DRIVER**, a livery stable chauffeur, Irish, slightly drunk. He is carrying a small rattan suitcase, which he puts down by the door. He is followed by **WALBECK**, forty-seven, prematurely gray; he speaks softly, but gives an impression of controlled power. **BERNICE** enters behind them.)*

WALBECK. *(to **MALLISON**, in a low voice)* I understood that the fare was paid in advance?

MALLISON. The twenty dollars was paid in advance.

DRIVER. Anybody'd charge twice to drive on a night like this. First it was rain and snow –

MALLISON. The livery stable was given twenty dollars – *(to **BERNICE**)* You can prepare the dinner!

*(Exit **BERNICE**.)*

DRIVER. Then it turned to ice. The worst night I've ever seen, to go to Joliet and pick up a I-don't-know-what. The car falling off the road every minute. To go to Joliet and pick up a criminal of some sort –

WALBECK. *(gesture of empty pockets)* I have no money.

MALLISON. *(to the* **DRIVER***)* I will give you five dollars, but I shall report you to the livery stable.

DRIVER. *(taking the bill)* What do I care? Thirty-five miles each way and half the time you couldn't see the road five yards in front of you; and the other half sliding into the ditch. All right, tell 'em and see what I tell 'em.

MALLISON. You have your five dollars. If you go now, I'll say nothing to your superiors – But go!

DRIVER. *(starting for the door, then turning on* **WALBECK***)* And who do you think you are, Mr. Bur-gessss! Keeping your mouth so shut! You a murderer or I-don't-know-what; and too big and mighty to talk to anybody. – Oh, you had to think, did you? So you had to think? Well, you've got enough to think about for the rest of your goddamned life.

(He goes out.)

MALLISON. *(stiffly)* Good evening, Mr. Walbeck.

(The front door is heard closing with a slam.)

WALBECK. *(always softly, but impersonally)* What is this name of...Burgess?

MALLISON. We assumed, Mr. Walbeck, that you would prefer us to engage the household staff and...make certain other arrangements under...another name. Since you did not reply to our letters on this matter, we selected the name of Burgess.

WALBECK. I see. – Is...my wife here?

MALLISON. *(astonished)* You did not get Mrs. Walbeck's letters?

WALBECK. I did not open any letters.

MALLISON. And our letters, Mr. Walbeck?

WALBECK. I haven't opened any letters for six months.

MALLISON. *(controlling his outrage, primly)* Mrs. Walbeck left a week ago – with the children – for California. She has filed a petition for divorce. In her letters she probably explained it to you at length. She did not wish to make this move earlier…She wished it to be known that she stood by you through…your ordeal. When she heard that your sentence had been reduced and that you would be returning this week, she –

WALBECK. *(coolly)* There's no need to say anything more, Mr. Mallison.

MALLISON. A woman has been engaged to attend to your needs. Her name is Bernice. A wardrobe – that is, a wardrobe of clothes – you will find upstairs. Your measurements were obtained by your former tailor from the authorities at the…institution from which you have come. – Here are the keys of the house. Here are the statements from your bank. A checkbook. Here *(He places a long envelope on the table.)* are five hundred dollars which I have drawn for your immediate needs.

WALBECK. Thank you. Good night.

MALLISON. Mr. Walbeck, hitherto the firm of Bremerton, Bremerton, Mallison and Mallison has been happy to serve as your legal representatives. From now on we trust that you will find other counsel. We relinquish – here *(He lays down another document.)* our power of attorney. And in this envelope you will find all the documents and information that our successors will require. I wish you good night.

WALBECK. *(stonily)* Good night.

(MALLISON turns at the door.)

MALLISON. You read no letters?

WALBECK. *(his eyes on the ground)* No.

MALLISON. That reminds me. Your daughter Lavinia wished to leave a letter for you. Her mother forbade her to do so. However, I…I was prepared to take the responsibility. Your daughter gave me this letter to give to you.

(He gives an envelope to **WALBECK**, *who puts it in his breast pocket. His silence and level glance complete* **MALLISON***'s discomfiture.)*

MALLISON. *(cont.)* Good night, sir.

(Exit **MALLISON**. **WALBECK** *stands motionless gazing fixedly before him. Suddenly, in a rage, he overturns the table before him; but immediately recovers his self-control. Enter* **BERNICE**.*)*

BERNICE. Dinner's served, sir.

WALBECK. I won't have any dinner.

BERNICE. Yes, Mr. Burgess.

WALBECK. What?

BERNICE. I said, "Yes, Mr. Burgess." I'll just set that table to rights.

WALBECK. *(quickly)* I'll do it.

(He does.)

BERNICE. *(watchfully but unsentimentally)* I've got a real good steak in there. I'm the best cook in Chicago, Mr. Burgess. There's lots of people that knows that.

WALBECK. Is there any liquor in the house?

BERNICE. Oh, yes. There's everything.

WALBECK. Rye. Rye straight. – You eat the steak.

BERNICE. Thank you, Mr. Burgess. *(she starts out, then turns)* Now, you don't want to eat that steak, Mr. Burgess, but I've got some tomato soup there that's the best tomato soup you ever ate. You aren't going to waste my time by refusing to eat that soup.

WALBECK. *(looking at her; impersonally)* What is your name?

BERNICE. My name's Bernice Mayhew. People calls me Bernice.

WALBECK. Bernice, I don't want to eat in that dining room. You can bring me the rye and some of that soup in here.

BERNICE. Yes, Mr. Burgess.

WALBECK. My name is Walbeck.

BERNICE. What's that?

WALBECK. My name: Wal-beck, Walbeck.

BERNICE. Yes, Mr. Walbeck.

WALBECK. And pour yourself some rye, Bernice.

BERNICE. I don't touch it, Mr. Walbeck. Ten years ago I made my life over. I changed my name and I changed everything about myself. I thank you, but I don't touch liquor.

(*She goes out.* **WALBECK,** *standing straight, his eyes on the ground, puts his hand in his pocket and draws out his daughter's letter. After a moment's hesitation, he opens it. He holds it suspended in his hand a moment. Then he tears the letter and envelope, each two ways, and throws the fragments into the fire [invisible to us], between the andirons.* **BERNICE** *returns, pushing a small service table. She gives him the rye, then unfurls a tablecloth and starts laying the table.* **WALBECK** *drinks half the rye in one swallow.*)

WALBECK. Were you here when my wife was here?

BERNICE. No, sir. Nobody's been here today but that lawyer-man. I came here this morning and all day Jason and I have been cleaning the house.

WALBECK. Do you know where I come from?

BERNICE. (*euietly, lowered eye*) Yes, I do.

WALBECK. Did that lawyer tell you?

BERNICE. No…I knew…I been there myself…So I knew. I'll get your soup.

(*She goes out. Suddenly* **WALBECK** *goes to the fireplace. Falling on his knees, he tries without burning his fingers to rake out the fragments of the letter. Apparently it is too late.* **BERNICE** *enters with a covered soup tureen. Watchfully, but with no show of surprise, she tries to take in what he is doing.* **WALBECK** *rises, dusting off his knees.*)

You want me to build up that fire, Mr. Walbeck?

WALBECK. No, it's all right as it is.

(He seats himself at the table.)

BERNICE. *(eyeing the fireplace speculatively)* There's some toast there, too.

WALBECK. You say you changed your name?

BERNICE. Yes. My born name was Sarah Temple. When I came out of prison I was Bernice Mayhew. Of course, I had some other names too. I was married twice. But Bernice Mayhew was the name I gave myself. *(without emphasis; her eyes on the distance)* I was in because I killed somebody.

WALBECK. *(the soup spoon at his mouth, speaks in her tone)* I was in because I cheated two or three hundred people out of money.

BERNICE. *(musingly)* Well, everybody's done something.

*(Pause. **WALBECK** eats.)*

WALBECK. You say you changed everything about yourself?

BERNICE. Yes. Everything was changed, anyway. I was in a disgrace – nobody can be in a bigger disgrace than I was. And some people were avoiding me and some people were laughing at me and some people were being kind to me, like I was a dog that came to the back door. And some people were saying cheer up, Sarah, you've paid your price. There's lots of things to live for. You're young yet. – You're sure you wouldn't like a piece of that steak, Mr. Walbeck, rare or any way you'd like it?

WALBECK. No. I'm going downtown soon. If I get hungry, later, I'll pick up something to eat down there.

BERNICE. *(after a short pause, while she continues to gaze into the distance)* Did anybody come to meet you when you came out of the door of the place you was at?

WALBECK. No.

BERNICE. That's what I mean. I don't blame them. I wouldn't want to go 'round with a person who's very much in a disgrace – like with a person who's killed somebody. I wouldn't choose 'em.

WALBECK. Or with a person who's stolen a lot of people's life savings.

BERNICE. I only mentioned that to show a big part of the change: you're alone.

WALBECK. Did that lawyer who was here, or the agency, know that you'd been in prison?

BERNICE. Oh, no. It was Sarah Temple who did that. She's dead. When I changed my name she became dead. You see the first part of my life I lived in Kansas City. Then I came to Chicago. Bernice Mayhew has never been to Kansas City. She don't even know what it looks like.

WALBECK. *(impersonally, without looking at her)* If you've been on your feet all day cleaning the house, I think you'd better sit down, Bernice.

BERNICE. Well, thank you, I will sit down.

WALBECK. Would you advise me to kill off George Walbeck?

BERNICE. *(seeming more and more remote, in her musings)* Not so much for your sake as for other people's sake. It's not good for other people to have to do with persons who are in a disgrace; it brings out the worst in them. I don't like to see that.

WALBECK. *(slowly, his eyes on the distance)* I guess you're right. I'd better do that.

BERNICE. It's like what happens about poor people. You're a thousand times richer than I am, but I'm richer than millions of people. What good does it do to think about them? I only need one real meal a day; the rest is just stuffing. But I don't notice as how I give up my other two meals. I'm always right there at mealtimes. When I went hungry, most times I didn't let people know about it; and when I'm in a disgrace, why should I make them uncomfortable?

WALBECK. Before you became Bernice Mayhew, did you have any children?

BERNICE. Yes, I did…Their mother's dead, of course. But I guess somebody's reminding them every day that their mother was a murderer. – That's bad enough, but it's not as bad as knowing their mother's alive. – Have you noticed that we gradually forgive them that's dead? If I was alive they'd be thinking about me, in one way or another hating me or maybe trying to stand up for me. There are a lot of ideas young people could go through about a thing like that.

WALBECK. *(as though to himself)* Yes.

(The telephone rings in the hall. **WALBECK** *rises uneasily.)*

Who could that be? Answer it, will you, Bernice? Don't say that I'm here.

*(***BERNICE*** goes into the hall. Her voice can be heard shouting as though she were unaccustomed to the telephone.)*

BERNICE. It's me talking – Bernice. Yes. Who are you, talking? Who? Oh. I can't understand much. A letter? I hear you, a letter. Yes, miss. What? I can't hear good. The machine don't work good. All right, you come. I'm here. Bernice. Yes, you come. I'm here.

*(***BERNICE*** returns to the stage.)*

She says she's your daughter.

WALBECK. So-o-o! She didn't go to California with her mother.

BERNICE. She says she sent you a letter. In the letter she asked you to telephone her…that she could come and see you. She was asking over and over again if you was here, but I made out that the machine didn't work good. She says she'll be here soon.

*(***BERNICE*** has been clearing the table, putting the objects on the wheeled service table, which she starts pushing to the door.)*

WALBECK. I can't see her tonight. – What do you suppose she wants?

BERNICE. *(at the door with lowered eyes)* I think I can figger that out about what half the daughters in the world would want. She wants to make a home for you. And to give up her life for you.

(She goes out with the service table.)

WALBECK. *(softly)* Good God – (**BERNICE** *returns and stands at the door.)* She's seventeen! How could she get such an idea! Her mother must have told her what she thought of me told her every day for eight years what she thought of me –

BERNICE. *(always without looking at him, broodingly)* Yes. *(slight pause)* Mr. Walbeck, you ought to know that women don't believe what women say. Least of all their mothers. They'll believe any old fool thing a man says.

WALBECK. She's seventeen! How did she do it? How did she get away from her mother? She must have run away at the railway station. She probably has very little money.

BERNICE. *("seeing" it; staring before her)* She's got some rings, hasn't she? She'll be selling them. She'll be going to the stores hunting for a job.

WALBECK. *(staring at her)* Yes. – But her mother will have come back to look for her. Or will have telephoned the police to look for her.

BERNICE. Maybe not. Maybe not at all…It's terrible when young girls are brave.

WALBECK. *(In a sort of terror. For the first time loudly.)* Bernice! – What shall I do?

BERNICE. *(a quick glance of somber anger)* It ain't right to ask advices. It ain't right, Mr. Walbeck.

WALBECK. See here, Bernice! Do this for me.

BERNICE. Do what, for you?

WALBECK. Do what you'd do, if it were your own daughter.

BERNICE. *(sudden flood of tormented emotion)* How do I know if I did right? – What I did about my own daughter? Maybe my daughter'd be having a good big life living with me. Maybe she's just having one of them silly lives, living with silly people and saying jabber – jabber silly things all day. *(gazing before her)* I hate people who don't know that lots of people is hungry and that lots of people has done bad things. If my daughter was with me, we'd talk …I got so many things I've *learned* that I could tell to a girl like that…And we'd go downtown and we'd shop for her clothes together…and talk… I've got a weak heart; I shouldn't get excited. *(She looks at the floor a minute.)* No, Mr. Walbeck, don't ask me to throw your daughter back into the trashy lives that most people live.

WALBECK. When she comes, give her her choice. I'll go upstairs.

BERNICE. Young people can't make choices. They don't know what they're choosing.

WALBECK. *(with increasing almost choked urgency)* Then tell her…she and I'll go away together. Somewhere. We'll start a new life.

*(**BERNICE** is silent a moment. Then her mood changes. For the first time she brings a long deep gaze toward him.)*

BERNICE. No! – These are just fancies. We're a stone around their necks now! If we were with them we'd be a bigger stone. Sometimes I think death come into the world so we wouldn't *be* a stone around young people's necks. Besides you and I – we're alone. We did what we did because we were that kind of person – the kind that chooses to think they're smarter and better than other people…And people that think that way end up alone. We're not *company* for anybody.

*(Pause. **WALBECK**'s mood also changes.)*

WALBECK. *(his mind made up)* Then tell her that the doctors told me that I had only a few months to live…that I've gone off so as not to be a weight on anybody…on her, for instance. *(He pulls the envelope from his pocket.)* If she's not followed her mother to California, she'll be needing some money. Give her this envelope. *(his tormented urgency returns)* And tell her…Tell her…

BERNICE. *(somberly but largely)* I knows what else to tell her, Mr. Walbeck. You go upstairs and hide youself. You's almost dead. You's dyin'.

(WALBECK goes out. BERNICE sits in a chair facing the audience, waiting, her eyes on the distance.)

End of Play

THREE

THE WRECK ON THE FIVE-TWENTY-FIVE

(Sloth)

CHARACTERS

MRS. HAWKINS, forty

MINNIE, her daughter, almost sixteen

MR. FORBES, a neighbor

MR. HERBERT HAWKINS, Mrs. Hawkins's husband

SETTING

Today. The Hawkins home.

(Six o'clock in the evening. **MRS. HAWKINS,** *forty, and her daughter* **MINNIE,** *almost sixteen, are sewing and knitting. At the back is a door into the hall and beside it a table on which is a telephone.)*

MRS. HAWKINS. Irish stew doesn't seem right for Sunday dinner, somehow. *(pause)* And your father doesn't really like roast or veal. *(pause)* Thank Heaven, he's not crazy about steak. *(another pause while she takes some pins from her mouth)* I must say it's downright strange – his not being here. He hasn't telephoned for years, like that – that he'd take a later train.

MINNIE. Did he say what was keeping him?

MRS. HAWKINS. No…something at the office, I suppose. *(She changes pins again.)* He never really did like chicken, either.

MINNIE. He ate pork last week without saying anything. You might try pork chops, Mama; I don't really mind them.

MRS. HAWKINS. He doesn't ever say anything. He eats what's there. – Oh, Minnie, men never realize that there's only a limited number of things to eat.

MINNIE. What did he say on the telephone exactly?

MRS. HAWKINS. "I'll try to catch the six-thirty."

(Both look at their wristwatches.)

MINNIE. But, Mama, Papa's not cranky about what he eats. He's always saying what a good cook you are.

MRS. HAWKINS. Men! *(She has put down her sewing and is gazing before her.)* They think they want a lot of change – variety and change, variety and change. But they don't really. Deep down, they don't.

MINNIE. Don't what?

MRS. HAWKINS. You know for a while he read all those wild Western magazines: cowboys and horses and silly Indians…two or three a week. Then, suddenly, he stopped all that. It's as though he thought he were in a kind of jail or prison. – Keep an eye on that window, Minnie. He may be coming down the street any minute.

(**MINNIE** *rises and, turning, peers through a window, back right.*)

MINNIE. No. – There's Mr. Wilkerson, though. He came back on the five-twenty-five, anyway. Sometimes Papa stops at the tobacco shop and comes down Spruce Street.

(*She moves to the left and looks through another window.*)

MRS. HAWKINS. Do you feel as though you were in a jail, Minnie?

MINNIE. What?!

MRS. HAWKINS. As though life were a jail?

MINNIE. (*returning to her chair*) No, of course not. – Mama, you're talking awfully funny tonight.

MRS. HAWKINS. I'm not myself. (*laughs lightly*) I guess I'm not myself because of your father's phone call – his taking a later train, like that, for the first time in so many years.

MINNIE. (*with a little giggle*) I don't know what the five-twenty-five will have done without him.

MRS. HAWKINS. (*not sharply*) And all those hoodlums he plays cards with every afternoon.

MINNIE. And all the jokes they make.

(**MRS. HAWKINS** *has been looking straight before her through a window – over the audience's heads, intently.*)

MRS. HAWKINS. There's Mrs. Cochran cooking her dinner.

(*They both gaze absorbedly at Mrs. Cochran a moment.*)

Well, I'm not going to start dinner until your father puts foot in this house.

MINNIE. *(still gazing through the window; slowly)* There's Mr. Cochran at the door…They're arguing about something.

MRS. HAWKINS. Well, that shows that he got in on the five-twenty-five, all right.

MINNIE. Don't people look foolish when you see them, like that – and you can't hear what they're saying? Like ants or something. Somehow, you feel it's not right to look at them when they don't know it.

(They return to their work.)

MRS. HAWKINS. Yes, those men on the train will have missed those awful jokes your father makes. *(MINNIE giggles)* I declare, Minnie, every year your father makes worse jokes. It's growing on him.

MINNIE. I don't think they're awful, but, I don't understand all of them. Do you? Like what he said to the minister Sunday. I was so embarrassed I didn't want to tell you.

MRS. HAWKINS. I don't want to hear it – not tonight. *(Her gaze returns to the window.)* I can't understand why Mrs. Cochran is acting so strangely. And Mr. Cochran has been coming in and out of the kitchen.

MINNIE. And they seem to keep looking at us all the time.

(After a moment's gazing, they return to their work.)

MRS. HAWKINS. Well, you might as well tell me what your father said to the minister.

MINNIE. I…I don't want to tell you, if it makes you nervous.

MRS. HAWKINS. I've lived with his jokes for twenty years. I guess I can stand one more.

MINNIE. Mr. Brown had preached a sermon about the atom bomb…and about how terrible it would be…and at the church door Papa said to him: "Fine sermon, Joe. I enjoyed it. But have you ever thought of this, Joe" he said – "suppose the atom bomb didn't fall, what would we do then? Have you ever thought of that?" Mr. Brown looked terribly put out.

MRS. HAWKINS. *(puts down her sewing)* He said that!! I declare, he's getting worse. I don't know where he gets such ideas. People will be beginning to think he's bitter. Your father isn't bitter. I know he's not bitter.

MINNIE. No, Mama. People like it. People stop me on the street and tell me what a wonderful sense of humor he has. Like...like... *(she gives up the attempt and says merely)* Oh, nothing.

MRS. HAWKINS. Go on. Say what you were going to say.

MINNIE. What did he mean by saying: "There we sit for twenty years playing cards on the five-twenty-five, hoping that something big and terrible and wonderful will happen – like a wreck, for instance?"

MRS. HAWKINS. *(more distress than indignation)* I say to you seriously, Minnie, it's just self-indulgence. We do everything we know how to make him happy. He loves his home, you know he does. He likes his work – he's proud of what he does at the office. *(She rises and looks down the street through the window at the back. Moved.)* Oh, it's not us he's impatient at: it's the whole world. He simply wishes the whole world were different – that's the trouble with him.

MINNIE. Why, Mama, Papa doesn't complain about anything.

MRS. HAWKINS. Well, I wish he would complain once in a while. *(she returns to her chair)* For Sunday I'll see if I can't get an extra good bit of veal. *(They sit in silence a moment. The telephone rings.)* Answer that, will you, dear? – No, I'll answer it.

(MINNIE returns to her work. MRS. HAWKINS has a special voice for answering the telephone, slow and measured.)

This is Mrs. Hawkins speaking. Oh, yes, Mr. Cochran. What's that? I don't hear you. *(a shade of anxiety)* Are you sure? You must be mistaken.

MINNIE. Mama, what is it?

*(*MRS. HAWKINS *listens in silence.)*

MINNIE. Mama! Mama!! – What's he saying? Is it about Papa?

MRS. HAWKINS. Will you hold the line one minute, Mr. Cochran? I wish to speak to my daughter. *(She puts her hand over the mouthpiece.)* No, Minnie. It's not about your father at all.

MINNIE. *(rising)* Then what is it?

MRS. HAWKINS. *(in a low, distinct and firm voice)* Now you do what I tell you. Sit down and go on knitting. Don't look up at me and don't show any surprise.

MINNIE. *(a groan of protest)* Mama!

MRS. HAWKINS. There's nothing to be alarmed about – but I want you to obey me. *(She speaks into the telephone.)* Yes, Mr. Cochran...No...Mr. Hawkins telephoned that he was taking a later train tonight. I'm expecting him on the six-thirty. You do what you think best. I'm not sure that's necessary but...you do what you think best. We'll be right here.

(She hangs up and stands thinking a moment.)

MINNIE. Mama, I'm almost sixteen. Tell me what it's about.

MRS. HAWKINS. *(returns to her chair; bending over her work, she speaks as guardedly as possible)* Minnie, there's probably nothing to be alarmed about. Don't show any surprise at what I'm about to say to you. Mr. Cochran says that there's been somebody out on the lawn watching us – for ten minutes or more. A man. He's been standing in the shadow of the garage, just looking at us.

MINNIE. *(lowered head)* Is that all!

MRS. HAWKINS. Well, Mr. Cochran doesn't like it. He's...he says he's going to telephone the police.

MINNIE. The police!!

MRS. HAWKINS. Your father'll be home any minute, anyway. *(slight pause)* I guess it's just some...some moody person on an evening walk. Maybe Mr. Cochran's done right to call the police, though. He says that we shouldn't pull the curtains or anything like that – but just act as though nothing has happened. – Now, I don't want you to get frightened.

MINNIE. I'm not, Mama. I'm just...interested. Most nights nothing happens.

MRS. HAWKINS. *(sharply)* I should hope not!

(slight pause)

MINNIE. Mama, all evening I did have the feeling that I was being watched...and that man was being watched by Mrs. Cochran; and *(slight giggle)* Mrs. Cochran was being watched by us.

MRS. HAWKINS. We'll know what it's all about in a few minutes.

(silence)

MINNIE. But Mama, what would the man be looking at? – Just us two sewing.

MRS. HAWKINS. I think you'd better go in the kitchen. Go slowly – and don't look out the window.

MINNIE. *(without raising her head)* No! I'm going to stay right here. But I'd like to know why a man would do that – would just stand and look. Is he...a crazy man?

MRS. HAWKINS. No, I don't think so.

MINNIE. Well, say something about him.

MRS. HAWKINS. Minnie, the world is full of people who think that everybody's happy except themselves. They think their lives should be more exciting.

MINNIE. Does that man think that our lives are exciting, Mama?

MRS. HAWKINS. Our lives are just as exciting as they ought to be, Minnie.

MINNIE. *(with a little giggle)* Well, they are tonight.

MRS. HAWKINS. They are all the time; and don't you forget it.

(The front door bell rings.)

Now, who can that be at the front door? I'll go, Minnie. *(weighing the dangers)* No, you go. – No, I'll go.

(She goes into the hall. The jovial voice of MR. FORBES *is heard.)*

MR. FORBES'S VOICE. Good evening, Mrs. Hawkins. Is Herb home?

MRS. HAWKINS'S VOICE. No, he hasn't come home yet, Mr. Forbes. He telephoned that he'd take a later train.

(Enter MR. FORBES, *followed by* MRS. HAWKINS.*)*

MR. FORBES. Yes, I know. The old five-twenty-five wasn't the same without him. Darn near went off the rails. *(to* MINNIE*)* Good evening, young lady.

MINNIE. *(head bent; tiny voice)* Good evening, Mr. Forbes.

MR. FORBES. Well, I thought I'd drop in and see Herb for a minute. About how maybe he'd be wanting a new car – now that he's come into all that money.

MRS. HAWKINS. Come into what money, Mr. Forbes?

MR. FORBES. Why, sure, he telephoned you about it?

MRS. HAWKINS. He didn't say anything about any money.

MR. FORBES. *(laughing loudly)* Well, maybe I've gone and put my foot in it again. So he didn't tell you anything about it yet? Haw-haw-haw. *(confidentially)* If he's got to pay taxes on it we figgered out he'd get about eighteen thousand dollars. – Well, you tell him I called, and tell him that I'll give him nine hundred dollars on that Chevrolet of his – maybe a little more after I've had a look at it.

MRS. HAWKINS. I'll tell him. – Mr. Forbes, I'm sorry I can't ask you to sit down, but my daughter's had a cold for days now and I wouldn't want you to take it home to your girls.

MR. FORBES. I'm sorry to hear that. – Well, as you say, I'd better not carry it with me. *(he goes to the door, then turns and says confidentially)* Do you know what Herb said when he heard that he'd got that money? Haw-haw-haw. I've always said Herb Hawkins has more sense of humor than anybody I know. Why, he said, "All window glass is the same." Haw-haw. "All window glass is the same." Herb! You can't beat him.

MRS. HAWKINS. "All window glass is the same." What did he mean by that?

MR. FORBES. You know: that thing he's always saying. About life. He said it at Rotary in his speech. You know how crazy people look when you see them through a window – arguing and carrying on – and you can't hear a word they say? He says that's the way things look to him. Wars and politics…and everything in life.

(**MRS. HAWKINS** *is silent and unamused.*)

Well, I'd better be going. Tell Herb there's real good glass – unbreakable – on the car I'm going to sell him. Good night, miss; good night, Mrs. Hawkins.

(*He goes out.* **MRS. HAWKINS** *does not accompany him to the front door. She stands a moment looking before her. Then she says, from deep thought.*)

MRS. HAWKINS. That's your father who's been standing out by the garage.

MINNIE. Why would he do that?

MRS. HAWKINS. Looking in. – I should have known it.

MINNIE. (*amazed but not alarmed*) Look! All over the lawn!

MRS. HAWKINS. The police have come. Those are their flashlights.

MINNIE. All over the place! I can hear them talking… (*pause*) …Papa's angry…Papa's very angry. (*they listen*) Now they're driving away.

MRS. HAWKINS. I should have known it. (*She returns to her seat. Sound of the front door opening and closing noisily.*) That's your father. Don't mention anything unless he mentions it first.

(*They bend over their work. From the hall sounds of* **HAWKINS** *singing the first phrase of "Valencia." Enter* **HAWKINS**, *a commuter. His manner is of loud, forced geniality.*)

HAWKINS. Well – HOW are the ladies?

(*He kisses each lightly on the cheek.*)

MRS. HAWKINS. I didn't start getting dinner until I knew when you'd get here.

HAWKINS. *(largely)* Well, don't start it. I'm taking you two ladies out to dinner. – There's no hurry, though. We'll go to Michaelson's after the crowd's thinned out. *(starting for the hall on his way to the kitchen)* Want a drink, anybody?

MRS. HAWKINS. No. The ice is ready for you on the shelf.

(He goes out. From the kitchen he can be heard singing "Valencia." He returns, glass in hand.)

What kept you, Herbert?

HAWKINS. Nothing. Nothing. I decided to take another train. *(He walks back and forth, holding his glass at the level of his face.)* I decided to take another train. *(He leans teasingly a moment over his wife's shoulder, conspiratorially.)* I thought maybe things might look different through the windows of another train. You know – all those towns I've never been in? Kenniston – Laidlaw – East Laidlaw – Bennsville. Let's go to Bennsville some day. Damn it, I don't know why people should go to Paris and Rome and Cairo when they could go to Bennsville. Bennsville! Oh, Bennsville –

MRS. HAWKINS. Have you been drinking, Herbert?

HAWKINS. This is the first swallow I've had since last night. Oh, Bennsville…breathes there a man with soul so dead –

*(**MINNIE**'s eyes have followed her father as he walks about with smiling appreciation.)*

MINNIE. I know a girl who lives in Bennsville.

HAWKINS. They're happy there, aren't they? No, not exactly happy, but they live it up to the full. In Bennsville they kick the hell out of life.

MINNIE. Her name's Eloise Brinton.

HAWKINS. Well, Bennsville and East Laidlaw don't look different through the windows of another train. It's not by looking through a train window that you can get at the heart of Bennsville. *(pause)* There all we fellows sit every night on the five-twenty-five playing cards and hoping against hope that there'll be that wonderful, beautiful –

MINNIE. *(laughing delightedly)* Wreck!!

MRS. HAWKINS. Herbert! I won't have you talking that way!

HAWKINS. A wreck, so that we can crawl out of the smoking, burning cars…and get into one of those houses. Do you know what you see from the windows of the train? Those people – those cars – that you see on the streets of Bennsville – they're just dummies. Cardboard. They've been put up there to deceive you. What really goes on in Bennsville – inside those houses – that's what's interesting. People with six arms and legs. People that can talk like Shakespeare. Children, Minnie, that can beat Einstein. Fabulous things.

MINNIE. Papa, I don't mind, but you make Mama nervous when you talk like that.

HAWKINS. Behind those walls. But it isn't only behind those walls that strange things go on. Right on that train, right in those cars. The damndest things. Fred Cochran and Phil Forbes –

MRS. HAWKINS. Mr. Forbes was here to see you.

HAWKINS. Fred Cochran and Phil Forbes – we've played cards together for twenty years. We're so expert at hiding things from one another – we're so cram-filled with things we can't say to one another that only a wreck could crack us open.

MINNIE. *(indicating her mother, reproachfully)* Papa!

MRS. HAWKINS. Herbert Hawkins, why did you stand out in the dark there, looking at us through the window?

HAWKINS. Well, I'll tell you…I got a lot of money today. But more than that I got a message. A message from beyond the grave. From the dead. There was this old lady – I used to do her income tax for her – old lady. She'd keep me on a while – God, how she wanted someone to talk to…I'd say anything that came into my head…I want another drink.

(He goes into the kitchen. Again we hear him singing "Valencia.")

MINNIE. *(whispering)* Eighteen thousand dollars!

MRS. HAWKINS. We've just got to let him talk himself out.

MINNIE. But Mama, why did he go and stand out on the lawn?

MRS. HAWKINS. Shh!

(HAWKINS returns)

HAWKINS. I told her a lot of things. I told her –

MINNIE. I know! You told her that everything looked as though it were seen through glass.

HAWKINS. Yes, I did. *(pause)* You don't hear the words, or if you hear the words, they don't fit what you see. And one day she said to me: "Mr. Hawkins, you say that all the time: why don't you do it?" "Do what?" I said. "Really stand outside and look through some windows." *(pause)* I knew she meant my own…Well, to tell the truth, I was afraid to. I preferred to talk about it. *(He paces back and forth.)* She died. Today some lawyer called me up and said she's left me twenty thousand dollars.

MRS. HAWKINS. Herbert!

HAWKINS. *(his eyes on the distance)* "To Herbert Hawkins, in gratitude for many thoughtfulnesses and in appreciation of his sense of humor." From beyond the grave… It was an order. I took the four o'clock home…It took me a whole hour to get up the courage to go and stand *(he points)* out there.

MINNIE. But Papa, you didn't see anything! Just us sewing!

(HAWKINS stares before him, then, changing his mood, says briskly.)

HAWKINS. What are we going to have for Sunday dinner?

MINNIE. I know!

HAWKINS. *(pinching her ear)* Buffalo steak?

MINNIE. No.

HAWKINS. I had to live for a week once on rattlesnake stew.

MINNIE. Papa, you're awful.

MRS. HAWKINS. *(putting down her sewing; in an even voice)* Were you planning to go away, Herbert?

HAWKINS. What?

MRS. HAWKINS. *(for the first time, looking at him)* You were thinking of going away.

HAWKINS. *(looks into his glass a moment)* Far away. *(then again putting his face over her shoulder teasingly, but in a serious voice)* There is no "away."…There's only "here." – Get your hats; we're going out to dinner. – I've decided to move to "here." To take up residence, as they say. I'll move in tonight. I don't bring much baggage. – Get your hats.

MRS. HAWKINS. *(rising)* Herbert, we don't wear hats any more. That was in your mother's time. – Minnie, run upstairs and get my blue shawl.

HAWKINS. I'll go and get one more drop out in the kitchen.

MRS. HAWKINS. Herbert, I don't like your old lady.

HAWKINS. *(turning at the door in surprise)* Why, what's the matter with her?

MRS. HAWKINS. I can understand that she was in need of someone to talk to. – What business had she trying to make you look at Minnie and me through windows? As though we were strangers. *(She crosses and puts her sewing on the telephone table.)* People who've known one another as long as you and I have are not supposed to see one another. The pictures we have of one another are inside. – Herbert, last year one day I went to the city to have lunch with your sister. And as I was walking along the street, who do you think I saw coming toward me? From quite a ways off? You! My heart stopped beating and I prayed – I prayed that you wouldn't see me. And you passed by without seeing me. I didn't want you to see me in those silly clothes we wear when we go to the city – and in that silly hat with that silly look we put on our face when we're in public places. The person that other people see.

HAWKINS. *(with lowered eyes)* You saw me – with that silly look.

MRS. HAWKINS. Oh, no. I didn't look long enough for that. I was too busy hiding myself. – I don't know why Minnie's so long trying to find my shawl.

(She goes out. The telephone rings.)

HAWKINS. Yes, this is Herbert Hawkins. – Nat Fischer? Oh, hello, Nat...Oh!...All right. Sure, I see your point of view...Eleven o'clock. Yes, I'll be there. Eleven o'clock.

(He hangs up. MRS. HAWKINS *returns wearing a shawl.)*

MRS. HAWKINS. Was that call for me?

HAWKINS. No. It was for me all right. – I might as well tell you now what it was about.

(he stares at the floor)

MRS. HAWKINS. Well?

HAWKINS. A few minutes ago the police tried to arrest me for standing on my own lawn. Well, I got them over that. But they found a revolver on me – without a license. So I've got to show up at court tomorrow, eleven o'clock.

MRS. HAWKINS. *(short pause; thoughtfully)* Oh...a revolver.

HAWKINS. *(looking at the floor)* Yes...I thought that maybe it was best...that I go away...a long way.

MRS. HAWKINS. *(looking up with the beginning of a smile)* To Bennsville?

HAWKINS. Yes.

MRS. HAWKINS. Where life's so exciting. *(suddenly briskly)* Well, you get the license for that revolver, Herbert, so that you can prevent people looking in at us through the window, when they have no business to. – Turn out the lights when you come.

End of Play

FOUR

A RINGING OF DOORBELLS

(Envy)

*This play became available through the research and editing
of F. J. O'Neil of manuscripts in the Thornton Wilder
Collection at Yale University.*

CHARACTERS

MRS. BEATTIE, sixty-five, crippled with arthritis
MRS. MCCULLUM, her housekeeper
MRS. KINKAID, a caller, forty-five
DAPHNE, Mrs. Kinkaid's daughter, eighteen

SETTING

The front room of Mrs. Beattie's small house in Mount Hope, Florida, circa 1939.

(*MRS. BEATTIE, sixty-five, crippled with arthritis, ill, of a bad color, but proud, stoical and every inch the "General's Widow," wheels herself carefully into the room in her invalid's chair. She comes to a halt beside her worktable and starts to spread out the material for her knitting. A ball of yarn falls to the ground. She eyes it resentfully. Presently, and with great precautions, she gets out of her chair, stoops over and retrieves the wool. She has just regained her seat in the chair when MRS. MCCULLUM, her housekeeper, can be heard offstage.*)

MRS. MCCULLUM. Mrs. Beattie, Mrs. Beattie! (*She puts her head in the door.*) I have the most extraordinary thing to tell you. I mean it's perfectly terrible. I'll put the groceries in the kitchen. (*She enters from the back, her hands full of parcels and herself breathless with excitement.*) – And they'll be here any minute! (*She comes to the front of the stage and peers through a window toward the right.*) They'll be coming down that street in a minute.

MRS. BEATTIE. Now, do catch your breath, Mrs. McCullum, and tell me calmly what you have to say.

MRS. MCCULLUM. I recognized them at once – both the mother and daughter. You won't believe what I have to tell you.

MRS. BEATTIE. (*calmly*) I think you'd better sit down.

MRS. MCCULLUM. But they'll be here any minute.

MRS. BEATTIE. Who'll be here?

MRS. MCCULLUM. These dreadful people…I know you won't want to see them. I'll just send them away.

MRS. BEATTIE. Did you get my medicine?

MRS. MCCULLUM. Yes, I did. – Here's the bottle. And here's the change. – There I was sitting in Mr. Goheny's drugstore – and *they* came in. – The medicine was two-forty; you gave me a ten-dollar bill. Here's…seven…sixty… The mother asked Mr. Goheny where Willow Street was…and asked him if Mrs. Beattie was in town!! And she asked him if Mrs. Brigham lived in Mount Hope, too. – You see, *that's* what she does; she goes to people's houses. – People that have been in the army. *High up* in the army.

MRS. BEATTIE. Did you cash my check?

MRS. MCCULLUM. (*fumbles in her handbag; brings out an envelope, which she gives to* **MRS. BEATTIE**) Yes, I did. Here it is. Mr. Spottswood sends his regards and hopes that you are feeling better. – Oh, Mrs. Beattie, they're just common adventuresses. Don't see them.

MRS. BEATTIE. (*she verifies the contents of the envelope; then says with decision*) Mrs. McCullum, I don't like fluster. Now, you go over there and sit by the piano; and you don't say a word until I've counted to five. – Then you tell me what this is all about – starting from the beginning.

(**MRS. MCCULLUM** *goes to the front of the stage and sits by an invisible piano, containing herself.* **MRS. BEATTIE**, *calmly adjusting her knitting and starting a row, slowly counts to five.*)

One…two…breathe tranquilly, Mrs. McCullum… three…four…Where did you first see or know about this mother and daughter?

MRS. MCCULLUM. I do want to apologize, Mrs. Beattie, for being so excited, but (*again peering through the window*) I wanted you –

MRS. BEATTIE. Yes, Mrs. McCullum. You first met them – ?

MRS. MCCULLUM. When I was working for Mrs. Ferguson in Winter Park two years ago, they came to the door. She said that her husband had been in the army under General Ferguson…in Panama…no, in Hawaii…and what good friends they'd been. They don't beg. I mean they don't *seem* to beg. She says that the daughter has a beautiful voice and that she hasn't the money to train this girl's beautiful voice. And the girl gets up to sing and she faints.

MRS. BEATTIE. What?

MRS. MCCULLUM. Mrs. Beattie, the girl gets up as though she's about to sing, but she doesn't sing. She crumples up and falls on the floor. And the mother tells a whole story about how they're starving, and Mrs. Ferguson gave her two hundred dollars. But that's not all. The next day Mrs. Ogilvie called Mrs. Ferguson on the telephone and said that these two adventuresses had called at her house and the girl had fainted and she gave them one hundred dollars.

MRS. BEATTIE. *(knitting impassively)* Thank you. Did Mrs. Ferguson and Mrs. Ogilvie remember the names of these people?

MRS. MCCULLUM. No…but this mother seemed to know *all about* General Ferguson and General Ogilvie…They go everywhere and get money.

MRS. BEATTIE. Now be quiet and let me think a minute! *(pause)* Do you remember their name?

MRS. MCCULLUM. *(peering out the window)* No, I'm sorry I don't. But Mrs. Ferguson looked it up in the army register and it was there.

MRS. BEATTIE. How old is the girl?

MRS. MCCULLUM. Well, that's the funny part about it. I think she must be all of eighteen, *now*, but her mother dresses her up as though she were much younger – so that she'll be more pathetic when she faints.

MRS. BEATTIE. Does the mother look like a lady?

MRS. MCCULLUM. Yes…pretty much.

MRS. BEATTIE. *(her eyes on* **MRS. MCCULLUM** *with a sort of sardonic brooding)* Think of how full their lives must be! – Full…occupied!

MRS. MCCULLUM. *(with a start)* What? What's that you said, Mrs. Beattie? *Occupied*! – But what they're doing is immoral.

MRS. BEATTIE. I'd exchange places with them *like that!*

MRS. MCCULLUM. You're in one of those moods when I don't begin to understand a word you *say!* Anyway, you're not going to see them, are you?

MRS. BEATTIE. *(calmly)* Of course, I'm going to see them. – Mrs. McCullum, will you kindly get the hot water bottle for my knees?

MRS. MCCULLUM. I'll do that right now. But they'll be here in a minute. Won't you let me wheel you into your bedroom and bring you the bottle there?

MRS. BEATTIE. In the first place, I don't like to be wheeled anywhere. And whether they come at once or later, I'd like the hot water bottle now.

MRS. MCCULLUM. *(starting)* Yes, Mrs. Beattie.

MRS. BEATTIE. One minute: tell me about the girl. She has lots of spirit. – Is this daughter pretty?

MRS. MCCULLUM. Yes. – Yes, she is…and that reminds me: will you excuse, Mrs. Beattie, if I make a suggestion?

MRS. BEATTIE. Yes, indeed, what is it?

MRS. MCCULLUM. Excuse me…but I think I should prepare you. The daughter – it struck me at once – resembles, very much resembles, that…dear photograph on the piano. I mean I couldn't help noticing it. Will you let me take the photograph into your bedroom?

MRS. BEATTIE. *(impassive, only her eyes concentrated)* I see no need to change anything in this room, Mrs. McCullum.

MRS. MCCULLUM. I'll get the hot water bottle.

(She goes out. Again **MRS. BEATTIE** *painfully descends from the chair. She moves to the piano and gazes long at the photograph. Then she moves farther forward on the stage and turns her head down the street. She sees the couple. She stares at them fixedly and somberly.* **MRS. MCCULLUM** *enters with a hot water bottle.)*

MRS. MCCULLUM. Mrs. Beattie! You're up!

*(***MRS. BEATTIE** *indicates with a gesture the couple up the street.* **MRS. MCCULLUM** *rushes to her side.)*

MRS. MCCULLUM. Yes! That's they. She has that sort of list in her hand she studies all the time. – Oh, let me send them away. They're just swindlers – common swindlers.

MRS. BEATTIE. Look! – She's studying her notes. – Yes, the girl – there is a resemblance…Isn't it strange…*(broodingly, with a touch of bitterness)* Young…and beautiful… occupied…

MRS. MCCULLUM. And wicked!

MRS. BEATTIE. *(dismissing this)* Oh!…Alive…*(starting to hobble off)* Alive and together…Bring them in here. Be very polite to them. Tell them I'm lying down. We'll make them wait a bit…If they don't have calling cards, get their names very carefully and bring them in to me…I'm going to receive them without my wheelchair.

MRS. MCCULLUM. Mrs. Beattie!

MRS. BEATTIE. And while they're waiting for me I'm going to ask you to bring some tea in to them.

MRS. MCCULLUM. *(looking out the window)* Oh! They're almost here!

MRS. BEATTIE. Alive and together – that's the point.

(She goes out.)

MRS. MCCULLUM. *(picking up her parcels and pushing the empty chair)* Why, Mrs. Beattie, you're better every day. You know you are.

(She is out.)

(The doorbell rings.)

(offstage) Mrs. Beattie? Yes. Will you come in, please? Who shall I say is calling?

(Enter MRS. KINKAID and DAPHNE. MRS. KINKAID is about forty-five, simply and tastefully dressed. She was once very pretty, but is now pinched, tense and unhappy. DAPHNE is eighteen, dressed for sixteen; she is cool, arrogant and sullen. MRS. KINKAID selects a calling card from her handbag.)

MRS. KINKAID. *(giving the card, without effusiveness)* Will you say Mrs. Kinkaid, the widow of Major George Kinkaid, a friend of General Beattie! And our daughter Daphne.

MRS. MCCULLUM. Mrs. Kin…kaid. Will you sit down, please. Mrs. Beattie is resting. I'll ask if she can see you.

MRS. KINKAID. Thank you.

MRS. MCCULLUM. There are some magazines here, if you wish to look at them.

MRS. KINKAID. Thank you.

(MRS. MCCULLUM goes out. The visitors sit very straight, scarcely turning their heads. Their eyes begin to appraise the room. When they speak, they move their lips as little as possible.)

DAPHNE. *(after a considerable pause, contemptuously)* Just junk.

MRS. KINKAID. The cabinet's very good. *(They both gaze at it appraisingly.)* When you fall, fall that side.

DAPHNE. We won't get fifty dollars.

MRS. KINKAID. And do that sigh – that sort of groan you did in Orlando. You've been forgetting to do that lately. Daphne! You've forgotten to take your wristwatch off. Really, you're getting awfully careless lately.

(DAPHNE removes her wristwatch and puts it in her handbag. She rises stealthily and goes tiptoe to the back and listens. MRS. KINKAID has taken a piece of notepaper from her handbag, but watches DAPHNE's movements anxiously. As DAPHNE continues to listen, MRS. KINKAID applies herself to the notes in her hand, murmuring the words as though for memorization.)

Manila, 1912 to 1913 with General Beattie and General Holabird…1907 to 1911…Do you remember Mrs. Holabird in West Palm Beach…The Presidio, 1910… Oh, dear…

DAPHNE. *(returning to her chair, cool)* Something's going to go wrong today.

MRS. KINKAID. *(deeply alarmed)* What do you mean, Daphne?

DAPHNE. I can always tell.

MRS. KINKAID. No. No…How can you tell?

DAPHNE. There's going to be all hell let loose. Like that time in Sarasota.

MRS. KINKAID. *(rising, passionately)* Then let's go. Let's go at once. If it's going to be like that, I can't stand it, I really can't.

DAPHNE. Sit down! Stop making a fool of yourself.

MRS. KINKAID. This is the last time. I cannot go on with this any longer.

DAPHNE. *(harshly)* Cork it, will you!

*(***MRS. KINKAID*** *sits down and sobs tonelessly into her handkerchief.)*

Of course, we've got to take risks. If we didn't take risks where'd we be? Do you want me to go back selling stockings?…I like risks…and if there's going to be trouble, I *like* it. I like talking back to these old witches…Pull yourself together and learn your stuff. *(pause)* Do you want to go back to that reception job in that hospital!?!

MRS. KINKAID. *(low, but intense)* Yes, I do, Daphne. Anything but this.

DAPHNE. Seventy a week! *(She again fixes her eyes on the cabinet.)* Yes, that's not bad. It could go with the table at Mrs. O'Hallohan's. And the rugs at the Krantzes.

MRS. KINKAID. West Point, twelve. West Point, twelve. – Daphne, if you do see there may be trouble, give me the signal. You get so furious you forget to give me the signals. – Schofield Barracks. General Wilkins…1909.

DAPHNE. *(eyebrows raised; she means she hears* **MRS. MCCULLUM** *coming)* Hickey!

(Enter **MRS. MCCULLUM** *carrying a tea tray.)*

MRS. MCCULLUM. Mrs. Beattie says she'll be happy to see you. She asked me to bring you some tea while you're waiting.

MRS. KINKAID. That's *very* kind, indeed. Isn't that kind of Mrs. Beattie, Daphne?

MRS. MCCULLUM. The marmalade's from our own oranges.

MRS. KINKAID. Imagine that? – I hope Mrs. Beattie is well. Mrs. Farnsborough spoke of her as...as convalescent.

MRS. MCCULLUM. Thank you, Mrs. Beattie's pretty well. *(silence)* Now, I think you have everything.

MRS. KINKAID. Indeed, yes. Thank you very much.

(MRS. MCCULLUM goes out. MRS. KINKAID looks at her daughter's face anxiously.)

DAPHNE. *(looking out into space, scarcely moving her lips)* Trouble!

MRS. KINKAID. *(almost trembling; pouring the tea)* The last time!

DAPHNE. Nonsense. Just do what you have to do and get it over.

MRS. KINKAID. You're very difficult, Daphne. You're cruel. – Well, there are only six more addresses in Florida... and that's *all.*

DAPHNE. *(blandly)* California's as full of them as blackberries.

MRS. KINKAID. We are *not* going to California.

(DAPHNE goes over to take her cup. She kisses her mother.)

DAPHNE. Poor dear mother! *(whispering)* You forget so easily: our house...our car...my wedding...

MRS. KINKAID. *(clasping her face)* Oh, I wish you were married, Daphne, and *this* were all over.

DAPHNE. Well, find me the *man*, dear. Do I ever meet any men?

MRS. KINKAID. Charles is such a nice young man.

DAPHNE. *(suddenly darkly irritated)* Are you *crazy*? Who's *he*? – Go back and study your notes. We've got to play our cards well today.

(MRS. KINKAID's eyes have fallen on the photograph on the piano.)

MRS. KINKAID. Daphne! Do you see what I see?

DAPHNE. What?

MRS. KINKAID. That photograph, dear.

DAPHNE. What?

MRS. KINKAID. ...The resemblance. It – it looks just like you.

DAPHNE. *(a casual glance)* No, it doesn't.

MRS. KINKAID. It's amazing. *(reopening her handbag)* I know who it is, too. *(reading some notes from a reference book)* "A daughter Lydia Westerveldt, born 1912, died 1930." She's beautiful. She hasn't your eyes, dear...but the shape and the hair: it's amazing.

*(***DAPHNE*** rises, stands before the photograph and gazes at it intently.)*

DAPHNE. Lydia...general's daughter...

"Miss Beattie, may I have the next dance?"...

"I'm so sorry, Lieutenant, but I've promised the next dance to Colonel Randolph."

"My daughter's away at finishing school. I don't know when she'll be back. She's staying with friends all over New England."

(turning to her mother, sharply) She has a wedding ring on.

MRS. KINKAID. Do come and sit down, dear.

DAPHNE. *(to the photograph)* Of course, I don't like her. She had everything she wanted. She didn't know what it was to know *nobody,* to have to spend all your time among common vulgar people, to skimp –

MRS. KINKAID. Daphne!

DAPHNE. ...and she didn't have to see her own mother insulted *(whirling about to face her mother)* like *you* were by Mrs. Smith.

MRS. KINKAID. Dear, I wasn't *insulted* –

DAPHNE. *(back at the photograph)* And you never knew what it was to be treated *just ghastly* by men, because you were poor; you didn't know anything. *(She spits at the picture.)* There! There!

MRS. KINKAID. *(has risen; keeping her voice)* Daphne, you stop that right now, and drink your tea. Sometimes I don't know what comes over you...

(**DAPHNE** *returns, grand and somber, to her chair.*)

I never taught you to say things like that.

DAPHNE. *(airily)* I don't like the way she looks at me. *(rendered pleasurably light-headed by her outburst)* I feel better. I'm glad I talked to her.... Mother-mousie, we're going to be very successful today. I feel it in my bones...and tonight we're going to a movie, and *you know which one. (She hears a noise in the hall.)* Hickey!

(*Both compose themselves for the entrance of* **MRS. BEATTIE**. **MRS. BEATTIE** *enters alone, walking with the greatest difficulty, but putting on a cordial smile.*)

MRS. BEATTIE. Mrs. Kinkaid, good afternoon. I am Mrs. Beattie. Don't get up, please.

MRS. KINKAID. *(rising)* Good afternoon, Mrs. Beattie. This is my daughter, Daphne.

MRS. BEATTIE. *(stopping and looking at her hard)* Good afternoon, Miss Kinkaid. Please sit down, both of you.

MRS. KINKAID. We want to thank you...for sending the tea. So kind.

MRS. BEATTIE. *(sitting down)* Mrs. McCullum tells me you knew my husband.

MRS. KINKAID. Mrs. Beattie...My husband, Major George Kinkaid, was in the Philippines at the same time as General Beattie. He was a lieutenant at that time – it was 1912 and 1913 – and probably had very little opportunity to meet the General, but he knew very well a number of the members of your husband's staff General Ferguson – then Colonel Ferguson; and Colonel Fosdick. (**MRS. BEATTIE** *nods*) I was not there at the time. I was very ill for a number of years and the doctors thought it inadvisable that I should make the trip to the Far East.

MRS. BEATTIE. Were you ever in the Far East?

MRS. KINKAID. No, I wasn't.

MRS. BEATTIE. *(to* **DAPHNE***)* And where were you born, Miss Kinkaid?

DAPHNE. *(slight pause)* In Philadelphia.

MRS. BEATTIE. *(turning back to* **MRS. KINKAID***)* I assume that there is something that you wish to see me about?

MRS. KINKAID. *(She makes a pause, and clutching her handbag begins to speak with earnest candor.)* There is, Mrs. Beattie – I am faced with a problem and I have called on you in the hope that you will give me some advice. My daughter, Daphne

(**MRS. BEATTIE** *turns her eyes on* **DAPHNE.***)*

is endowed with a most unusual singing voice. Qualified musicians have told me that she has indeed an extraordinary voice. And in addition to that voice, a deeply musical nature. Professor Boncianiani of New York, who is recognized as one of the leading teachers, has predicted a great career for her. Perhaps, if you wish – a little later – I shall ask Daphne to sing for you. My problem is this – where will I find the means to cultivate her voice? So far I have been barely able to afford a certain amount of instruction…naturally, in a very modest way. *(she pauses)*

MRS. BEATTIE. I see. You draw a pension, of course.

MRS. KINKAID. No, Mrs. Beattie, I do not.

(She takes a handkerchief from her handbag.) I do not. My husband's career in the army began most promisingly. I have here letters from his superior officers expressing the highest opinion of his work. But my husband had…a weakness. *(She touches the handkerchief to her nose.)* I find this very hard to say…he was intemperate…

MRS. BEATTIE. I beg your pardon?

MRS. KINKAID. Somehow…alone in the Far East…he took to drinking. And on one occasion…under the influence of alcohol…he forgot himself…He was, I believe, impertinent to a superior officer…

MRS. BEATTIE. To whom?

MRS. KINKAID. To General Foley.

(Pause. **MRS. KINKAID** *dries her eyes.)*

MRS. BEATTIE. How have you made your living, Mrs. Kinkaid?

MRS. KINKAID. For a while I assisted in a small dress shop in Miami Beach. Then I was a receptionist in a hotel.

MRS. BEATTIE. And now?

MRS. KINKAID. I have not come to you with any problem about our livelihood, Mrs. Beattie. I hope to be able to sustain ourselves; it is Daphne's career – her God – given voice – that I feel to be my responsibility. – I would like you to hear Daphne sing. She is able to accompany herself. *(She looks inquiringly at* **MRS. BEATTIE** *who remains silent.)* Daphne, do that French song.

*(***DAPHNE** *has felt* **MRS. BEATTIE***'s weighted glance.)*

DAPHNE. Mother, I don't feel like singing. I think we should thank Mrs. Beattie for the tea and go.

MRS. KINKAID. Do make an effort, Daphne. Mrs. Beattie has been so kind.

*(***DAPHNE** *turns and looks at* **MRS. BEATTIE** *who meets her gaze.)*

DAPHNE. *(under her breath)* Mrs. Beattie has not asked me to sing.

MRS. BEATTIE. I should very much like to hear you sing, Miss Kinkaid.

DAPHNE. *(rising)* Very well, I will.

MRS. BEATTIE. *(distinctly)* It will not be necessary to faint.

MRS. KINKAID. *(bridling)* To faint!?

MRS. BEATTIE. It will not be necessary to faint. I have understood the problem. – Sit down, Miss Kinkaid. *(turning to* **MRS. KINKAID***, with decision)* How much of what you have told me is true?

MRS. KINKAID. *(rising; with indignation)* I do not know what you mean. I have never been spoken to in such a way. Come with me, Daphne. *(to **MRS. BEATTIE**)* Every word I have said is *true*.

*(**MRS. BEATTIE** remains impassive, her eyes on **DAPHNE**, who has not moved from where she stopped on her way to the piano.)*

MRS. BEATTIE. I shall not telephone the police unless you force me to.

MRS. KINKAID. *(about at the door)* The police! We have done nothing that concerns the police.

MRS. BEATTIE. They could ask you to give an account of the money you have received. – Have you an unusual voice, Miss Kinkaid?

DAPHNE. *(beginning with low contempt)* Oh, you can talk. You don't know what other people's lives are like. Our lives are just awful. You've got everything you want and you've always had everything you want. You don't know what it is for me to see my mother treated just like dirt by people she shouldn't even have to speak to.

MRS. KINKAID. Daphne! You know I've never complained –

DAPHNE. And everybody else has *cars*...and when they eat they eat things fit to eat. You don't know what it is to see your own mother –

*(**MRS. MCCULLUM** has come to the door.)*

MRS. MCCULLUM. Mrs. Beattie, you remember what the doctor said...You're not to have any excitement. I must ask these ladies to go.

MRS. BEATTIE. *(raising her hand)* I wish to hear what they have to say.

MRS. KINKAID. *(comes forward as if there had been no interruption)* Daphne has not expressed our intention correctly. Daphne is a very imaginative child and is given to exaggeration. I have never made any complaint about our lives, as far as I am concerned; but you cannot know what it is, Mrs. Beattie, to bring up a refined and sensitive girl like Daphne...without money and without...any social situation. The only girls and young men we have any opportunity to meet are coarse, and vulgar...often unspeakably vulgar. Daphne's place is among ladies and gentlemen. I have spent sleepless nights – many sleepless nights – trying to find some way to better our situation.

DAPHNE. *(now going to the door)* Come, Mother, she doesn't know what we're talking about. She was born igno-rant...and her daughter went from one dance to another dance...and her children would have the same thing. And what right did you have to a life like that? None at all. You were born into the right cradle. That's all you did to earn it.

MRS. BEATTIE. *(firmly but not sharply to* DAPHNE*)* Have you a remarkable voice?

DAPHNE. No.

MRS. KINKAID. Daphne!

[*(*MRS. BEATTIE *and* DAPHNE *look at one another.* MRS. KINKAID *and* MRS. MCCULLUM *are frozen where they stand.* MRS. BEATTIE *glances at* MRS. KINKAID *and then toward the antique cabinet on which stand the telephone and a writing kit with a pen holder and a checkbook. She moves carefully to the cabinet and pauses as if coming to an important decision.)*]

MRS. BEATTIE. [Alive and together...that's the point.]

[*(*MRS. BEATTIE *picks up the pen and checkbook and turns back to face* DAPHNE *and* MRS. KINKAID*, as the lights fade)*]

End of Play

A NOTE ON THE TEXT

This play became available through the research and editing of F. J. O'Neil of manuscripts in the Thornton Wilder Collection at Yale University. In June 1957, Thornton Wilder wrote in his journal that *In Shakespeare and the Bible* and *A Ringing of Doorbells* were plays he could "terminate any day, but which will never be finished."[1] The author's manuscript of *A Ringing of Doorbells* ended abruptly with this exchange:

MRS. BEATTIE. *(firmly but not sharply to* **DAPHNE***)* Have you a remarkable voice?

DAPHNE. No.

MRS. KINKAID. Daphne!

MRS. BEATTIE.

Just how "terminated" is the play? The answer would appear to be: all but Mrs. Beattie's last line. After dinner one evening at his home in Hamden, Connecticut, Thornton Wilder read aloud to me a nearly complete draft of this play and spoke of his plan to bring the story to a logical, but unconventional, conclusion. Mrs. Beattie, as envious of the Kinkaids as they are of her, wants to help them in spite of their attempt to trick her. A fair solution then to the missing last line seemed to be a reprise of Mrs. Beattie's earlier line:"Alive and together...that's the point," as her summing up at the point of decision. The stage directions that I added are consistent with what appears to be Wilder's intention. Combining the antique cabinet and the telephone, both already established in the text, with a writing kit and checkbook, allows a moment of suspense as Mrs. Beattie moves toward the desk, and then a final tableau as she turns back to face the Kinkaids, checkbook in hand.

F. J. O'Neil
April, 1997

---

1. *The Journals of Thornton Wilder 1939-1961*, entry 749, page 266, selected and edited by Donald Gallup, Yale University Press, 1985.

FIVE

IN SHAKESPEARE AND THE BIBLE

(Wrath)

This play became available through the research and editing of F. J. O'Neil of manuscripts in the Thornton Wilder Collection at Yale University.

CHARACTERS

MARGET, a maid

JOHN LUBBOCK, a young attorney, twenty-seven, Katy Buckingham's
    fiancé

MRS. MOWBREY, Katy Buckingham's aunt, late fifties

KATY BUCKINGHAM, twenty-one

SETTING

An oversumptuous parlor, New York, 1898.

*(All we need see are three chairs, a low sofa and a tab-
oret. Two steps descend from the hall at the back into
the room. A Swedish maid,* **MARGET**, *introduces* **JOHN
LUBBOCK**, *twenty-seven, self-assured; face and bearing
under absolute control.)*

LUBBOCK. Mrs. Mowbrey wrote me, asking me to call. My
name is Lubbock.

MARGET. Yes, sir. Mrs. Mowbrey is expecting you. She will
be down in a moment, sir. She says I'm to bring you
some port. I'll go and get it.

(Exit **MARGET**. **LUBBOCK**, *hands in his pockets, whistl-
ing under his breath, strolls about examining closely, one
by one, the pictures hanging on the wall invisible to us.*
MARGET *returns bearing a small tray on which are two
decanters and two goblets. She puts them on the taboret.)*

There's port in this one, sir, and sherry in this. Mrs.
Mowbrey says you're to help yourself.

LUBBOCK. Thank you. *(still examining the pictures)* These are
relatives and ancestors of Mrs. Mowbrey?

MARGET. Oh, yes. Mrs. Mowbrey comes of a very fine family.
I've heard her say that that is her father. As you can
see, a clergyman.

LUBBOCK. *(casually)* She lives alone here?

MARGET. Oh, yes. She's a widow, poor lady. And very much
alone. Would you believe it, if I said that no one's
come to the house to call for the whole time I've been
here, except her lawyer man. And, oh yes, the minister
of her church.

LUBBOCK. For several months.

MARGET. Oh, I've been here about a year. But today we're going to have two callers – you, sir, and a young lady that's coming later. Yes, and I mustn't forget when the doorbell rings for the young lady, I'm to take out the decanters before I open the door. Now I mustn't forget that. And then I'm to bring in the tea. Now, you'll help yourself, won't you?

(**MARGET** *goes out.* **LUBBOCK**, *thoughtfully, pours himself a considerable amount of sherry and, sipping it, returns to his examination of the room and the pictures. Enter* **MRS. MOWBREY**, *late fifties, handsome, florid, powdered. She wears a black satin dress covered with bugles and jet. She addresses* **LUBBOCK** *from the hall before descending into the room.*)

MRS. MOWBREY. Mr. Lubbock, I am Mrs. Mowbrey.

LUBBOCK. Good afternoon, ma'am.

MRS. MOWBREY. You don't know who I am?

LUBBOCK. No, ma'am. I got your letter asking me to call.

MRS. MOWBREY. (*coming forward*) Won't you sit down?

(*They sit,* **MRS. MOWBREY** *behind the taboret.*)

Mr. Lubbock, I had two reasons for asking you to call today. In the first place, I wish to engage a lawyer. I thought we might take a look at one another and see if we could work together. (*She pauses. He bows his head slightly and impersonally.*) I mean a lawyer to handle my affairs in general and to advise me. (*same business*) My second reason for asking to see you is that I am your fiancée's aunt.

LUBBOCK. (*amazed*) Miss Buckingham's aunt! She never told me she had an aunt.

MRS. MOWBREY. No, Mr. Lubbock, she wouldn't. I am the black sheep of the family. My name is not mentioned in that house. – Will you pour me some port, please. I am glad to see that you have helped yourself…Thank you…Yes, I am your future mother-in-law's sister.

(*He is standing up, holding his glass – waiting.*)

MRS. MOWBREY. *(cont.)* Our lives took different directions.

(He sits down.)

But before we get into the legal matter, let's get to know one another a little better. – Tell me, I haven't seen my niece for fifteen years. Is she a pretty girl?

LUBBOCK. Yes – very.

MRS. MOWBREY. We're a good-looking family.

LUBBOCK. *(indicating the pictures on the wall)* And a distinguished one. Miss Buckingham would be very interested in seeing these family portraits.

MRS. MOWBREY. Yes. *(she sips her wine, then says dryly, without a smile)* It's not hard to find family portraits, Mr. Lubbock. There are places on Twelfth Street, simply full of them. Bishops and generals – whatever you want.

LUBBOCK. *(continuing to look at them, also without a smile)* Very fine collection, I should say.

(She takes another sip of wine.)

MRS. MOWBREY. Mr. Lubbock, I've made some inquiries about you. You are twenty-seven years old.

LUBBOCK. Yes, I am.

MRS. MOWBREY. You took your time finding yourself, didn't you? All that unpleasantness down in Philadelphia. What happened exactly? Well, we won't go into it. Then you gave yourself a good shaking. You pulled yourself together. Law school – very good. People are still wondering where you got all that spending money. It wasn't horse racing. It wasn't cards. No one could figure it out. Apparently it was something you were doing up in Harlem. – Certainly, your parents couldn't afford to give you anything. In fact, you were very generous to them. You bought them a house on Staten Island. You were a very good son to them and I think you'll make a very good family man.

LUBBOCK. *(with a slight how and a touch of dry irony)* You are very well informed, ma'am.

MRS. MOWBREY. Yes, I am. *(She takes another sip of wine.)* On Saturday nights you often went to 321 West Street "The Palace," you boys called it. Nice girls, everyone of them, especially Dolores.

LUBBOCK. *(mastering violence; rises)* I don't like this conversation, ma'am. I shall ask you to let me take my leave.

MRS. MOWBREY. *(raising her voice)* You and I have met before, Mr. Lubbock. You knew me under another name. I owned The Palace.

LUBBOCK. Mrs. Higgins!!

MRS. MOWBREY. My hair is no longer blond. *(She rises and crosses the room.)* You may leave any moment you wish, but I never believed you were a hypocrite.

LUBBOCK. *(after returning her fixed gaze wrathfully; then sitting down again)* What do you want?

MRS. MOWBREY. Yes, I owned The Palace and several other establishments – refined, very refined in every way. I've sold them. I've retired. I see no one – no one – whom I knew in those days. Except today I am seeing yourself. Naturally, I am never going to mention these matters again. I am going to forget them, and I hope that you will forget them, too. But it would be very valuable to me to have a lawyer who knew them and who was in a position to forget them. – I'll have a little more port, if you'll be so good.

*(**LUBBOCK** takes the glass from her hand in silence, fills it at the taboret and carries it to her. She murmurs: "Thank you." He returns and stands by the taboret, talking to her across the length of the stage.)*

LUBBOCK. I don't believe you asked me here to engage me as your lawyer. There's something else on your mind. will you say it and then let me take my leave?

MRS. MOWBREY. You were always like that, Jack.

LUBBOCK. *(loud)* I will ask you not to call me Jack.

MRS. MOWBREY. *(bowing her head slightly)* That was always your way, Mr. Lubbock. Suspicious. Quick to fight. Imagining that everybody was trying to take advantage of you.

LUBBOCK. What do you want? I don't know what you're talking about. *(he starts with fuming lowered head for the door)* Good afternoon.

MRS. MOWBREY. Mr. Lubbock, I will tell you what I want. *(he pauses with his back to her)* I am a rich woman and I intend to get richer. And I am a lonely woman, and I don't think that that is necessary. I want to live. And when you and Katy are married, I want you to help me. *(he is "caught" and half turns)* I want company. I want to entertain. I also want to help people. I want – so to speak – to adopt some. Not young children, of course, but young men and women who want bringing out in some way or other. I have a gift for that kind of thing. – Even in my former work I was able to do all sorts of things for my girls. – Did you ever hear anyone say that Mrs. Higgins was mean – unkind – to the girls in her place?

(He refuses to answer; the port is going to her head. She strikes her bosom emotionally.)

I'm kind to a fault. I love to see young people happy. Dozens of those girls – I helped them get married. I encouraged them to find good homes. Against my own interest. – Your friend, Dolores married a policeman. Happy as a lark. *(She puts a delicate lace handkerchief to her eyes and then to her nose.)* – Will you consent to be my lawyer?

LUBBOCK. *(scorn and finality)* My firm doesn't allow us to serve family connections.

MRS. MOWBREY. Oh, I don't want to have anything to do with that wretched firm Wilbraham, Clayton, what's-its-name? All you do for me will be on your own time. I shall start giving you three thousand a year for your advice. Then –

LUBBOCK. I beg your pardon. It's entirely out of the question.

MRS. MOWBREY. *(after a slight pause; in a less emotional voice)* Yes, yes. I know that you are always ready with your no! no! You haven't yet heard what I can do for you. And I don't mean in the sense of money. There is something you are greatly in need of... *(pause)* ...John Lubbock. One can see that you are a lawyer – and a very good one, I suspect. – So, you looked about you and you selected my niece?

LUBBOCK. Oh, much more than that. I'm very much in love with your niece. You should know her. Katy's an extraordinary girl.

MRS. MOWBREY. Is she? There's nothing very extraordinary about her mother? What's extraordinary about Katy?

LUBBOCK. Why, she's...I feel that I'm the luckiest man in the world.

MRS. MOWBREY. Come now, Mr. Lubbock. You don't have to talk like that to me.

LUBBOCK. *(earnestly)* I assure you, I mean it.

MRS. MOWBREY. *(a touch of contempt)* Very clever, is she? Reads a lot of books and all that kind of thing?

LUBBOCK. No-o. *(with a slight laugh)* But she asks a lot of questions.

MRS. MOWBREY. *(pleased)* Does she? So do I, Mr. Lubbock, as you have noticed. *(She rises and starts toward her former seat by the decanter of port.)* She asks lots of questions. I like that. – I asked her to call this afternoon.

LUBBOCK. *(startled and uneasy)* You did? Did you tell her that I would be here?

MRS. MOWBREY. No. I thought I would surprise her.

LUBBOCK. Katy doesn't like surprises. *(preparing to leave, with hand outstretched)* I think that at your first meeting with – after so long a time – you should see her alone. Perhaps I can call on you at another time.

MRS. MOWBREY. *(still standing)* What are you so nervous about? It's not time for her to come yet, and besides I have this law matter to discuss with you.

LUBBOCK. Thank you. – I'll ask if I can call some other time.

MRS. MOWBREY. Anyway, perhaps she won't come. She'll have shown my letter to her mother and her mother will have forbidden her to come. Would Katy disobey her mother?

LUBBOCK. Yes.

MRS. MOWBREY. *(eyeing him)* Has Katy chosen to marry you against her mother's wishes?

LUBBOCK. Yes. Very much so.

MRS. MOWBREY. I see. Tears? Scenes? Slamming of doors?

LUBBOCK. Yes, I think so.

MRS. MOWBREY. *(leaning toward him confidentially, lifted finger)* Katy is like me, Mr. Lubbock. I can feel it with every word you say.

(Still uneasy, **LUBBOCK** *has been taking a few steps around the room; he looks up at the ceiling and weighs this thoughtfully.)*

LUBBOCK. If you told her you were her aunt…Yes, I think she will come. Katy likes to know…where she stands; what it's all about, and that kind of thing.

MRS. MOWBREY. I see. A lawyer's wife. As you suggested a few moments ago: she's inquisitive?

LUBBOCK. *(with a nervous laugh)* Yes, she is.

MRS. MOWBREY. And you think I'm inquisitive, too – don't you?

LUBBOCK. Yes, I do.

MRS. MOWBREY. Well, let me tell you something, Mr. Lubbock. Everybody says we women are inquisitive. Most of us are. We have to be. I wouldn't give a cent for a woman who wasn't. And why? *(The wine has gone to her head. She emphasizes what she is about to say by tapping with jeweled rings on the taboret.)* Because a good deal is asked of us for which we are not prepared. Women have to keep their wits about them to survive at all, Mr. Lubbock. *(She leans back in her chair.)* When I was married I didn't hesitate to read every scrap of paper my husband left lying around the house. But *(She leans forward.)* as I said, I have some business to discuss with you before Katy comes. – Do you always walk about that way?

LUBBOCK. *(surprised)* People tell me I do. I do in court. If it makes you uneasy –

MRS. MOWBREY. I would like to ask another thing. When you are married – and as a wedding present I shall give Katy a very large check, I assure you – I want you both to give me the opportunity to meet some of your friends, young people in whom I could take an interest. New York must be full of them. But most of all I want to see you two. I want you to feel that this house is your second home. *(very emotional)* I will do everything for you. I have no one else in the world. I will do everything for you. *(Again she puts her handkerchief to her face.)* Now I've talked a good deal. Have you anything to say to all this?

LUBBOCK. *(after rising and taking a few steps about)* Mrs. Mowbrey, I like people who talk frankly, as you do, and who go straight to the point. And I'm going to be frank with you. There's one big hitch in what you propose.

MRS. MOWBREY. Hitch?

LUBBOCK. Katy. *(He looks directly at her and repeats.)* Katy. Naturally, she wouldn't have anything to say about my professional life. – And I want to thank you for the confidence you express in my ability to be of service to you. *(He looks up at the ceiling in thought.)* But about those other points I don't know. I tell you frankly, Mrs. Mowbrey, I'm in love with Katy. I'm knocked off my feet by Katy. But I feel that I don't know her. How can I put it? I'm…I'm even afraid of Katy.

MRS. MOWBREY. *(almost outraged)* What? A man like you, afraid of a mere girl!

LUBBOCK. *(short laugh)* Well, perhaps that's going too far; but I swear to you I still can't imagine what it will be like to be married to Katy. *(His manner changes and he goes to her briskly as though to shake her hand.)* Really, I think it's best that I say good night now. Katy will want to see you alone. So I'll thank you very much and say good-bye. And ask if I may call on you at some other time.

MRS. MOWBREY. Nonsense! What possible harm could there be – ? *(the doorbell rings)* There! That's the doorbell. That's Katy. It's too late to go now. Do calm down, Mr. Lubbock.

*(enter **MARGET**)*

MARGET. That's the front door bell, Mrs. Mowbrey. Shall I take out the tray?

MRS. MOWBREY. Yes, Marget. And be quick about it.

*(**MARGET** scutters out with the tray.)*

Really, I don't understand you, Mr. Lubbock. This is not like you at all. There's nothing to get nervous about. The young girls of today are perfect geese – don't I know them! Pah!

*(**MARGET** at the door)*

MARGET. Miss Buckingham to see you, ma'am.

*(**KATY**, twenty-one, very pretty, stands a moment at the top step and looks all about the room.)*

MRS. MOWBREY. *(throwing her arms wide, without rising)* Ah, there you are, dear.

KATY. *(taking a few steps forward, her eyes on **LUBBOCK**)* Aunt Julia, I'm very glad to see you.

MRS. MOWBREY. *(apparently expecting to he kissed)* This is a joy!

*(**KATY**, approaching her, looks at her smiling, and suddenly drops her reticule which she has opened. Thus avoiding an embrace, she leans over and takes some time picking the objects up. **LUBBOCK** and **MARGET** come to her assistance.)*

KATY. Oh, how awkward of me! I'm so sorry. I'm always doing things like this. Thank you. There's my key... and my card case. Thank you.

MRS. MOWBREY. Marget, we're ready for tea now. I'm sure you'll want some tea, dear.

(*exit* **MARGET**)

KATY. Thank. you, I would. – You're here, John?

LUBBOCK. (*uncomfortable*) Mrs. Mowbrey wrote me and asked me to call.

MRS. MOWBREY. Yes, dear, I've wanted a lawyer so badly. Now sit down and let me look at you.

(**KATY** *sits in the chair* **MRS. MOWBREY** *has indicated.*)

What a dear, beautiful girl you are! – And you're so like my father! You're like me and my father.

LUBBOCK. (*reluctantly*) Yes...There is something there.

MRS. MOWBREY. Oh, I've lost my looks – I know that! I've been through great unhappiness, but the resemblance is there, there's no doubt about it.

KATY. Did you know I was coming, John?

LUBBOCK. No, no.

KATY. Is John going to be your lawyer, Aunt Julia?

MRS. MOWBREY. I hope so, dear. I certainly hope he will be. That'll bring us all closer and closer together.

KATY. Aunt Julia...I scarcely remember you. Why...why haven't we seen you more often?

MRS. MOWBREY. Mildred, dear, your mother and I...let's not talk about it. I'll just say this: sometimes in families, there are people who simply can't get on together. I hope your mother's happy. I wish her every good thing in the world. If she doesn't wish to see me, that doesn't change anything. I wish her every good thing in the world. You can tell her that any time you wish, Mildred. – But Mr. Lubbock tells me you wish to be called Kate?

KATY. Yes, I do.

MRS. MOWBREY. But why?

KATY. *(after looking down a moment)* That would take too long to explain, Aunt Julia.

MRS. MOWBREY. Well, you are a dear original girl, aren't you?

KATY. John, are you Aunt Julia's lawyer?

MRS. MOWBREY. He *will* be. He will be. We've just settled that. So that both my business and my pleasure – my affection, let us hope – will be close together. Oh, here's the tea.

(enter **MARGET** *with the tea service)*

Oh, I have such plans for you. Cream and sugar – both of you?

KATY & LUBBOCK. Thank you.

MRS. MOWBREY. You see, dear, I've lived too much alone, since my dear husband's death. That's not good. That's not right. And you are going to bring me out. – Now tell me, Katy, where are you going to live? Have you found just what you wanted?

KATY. Yes, we have. – Thank you.

MRS. MOWBREY. Splendid! Tell me, dear, don't have a moment's hesitation…What will it be: linen? silver?

KATY. Aunt Julia, I don't like receiving presents. I never have. I may be strange in that, but…I don't.

MRS. MOWBREY. Presents! But I'm your aunt – this is the family.

KATY. *(clearly)* But we don't know one another very well yet.

*(***MRS. MOWBREY*** is stopped short. She fumbles with her handkerchief. She begins silently to weep.)*

Have you been living in New York, Aunt Julia?

MRS. MOWBREY. That was not kind, Mildred. That was not kind.

KATY. *(searching herself, softly)* I'm sorry. I'm sorry, if…I think I'm supposed to be a very outspoken person, Aunt Julia, but I didn't mean to be unkind.

MRS. MOWBREY. *(still drying one eye; but in a low firm tone of instruction)* That means you must have been hurt in life, in some way. I've seen it often.

KATY. *(another glance at John, slowly)* No, I...don't think I have.

LUBBOCK. *(floundering, but trying to do his part)* Katy's right, Mrs. Mowbrey. But when she does make a friend, she's a real one.

MRS. MOWBREY. *That* I believe. And so am I. And I want to prove it to you. I want you to come to feel that this is your second home. I want to be useful to you, in any way. Do you know, Katy, that when I was a girl *I* changed my name, too? I was christened Julia; but I didn't like it. I wanted a name out of the Bible. I liked the story of Esther. I liked her courage. That's what I like: courage. Now will you tell me why you changed yours?

KATY. Well...I used to read Shakespeare all the time. And I liked the girls in Shakespeare. Even when I was very young...Every day I'd pretend I was a different one. And, you know, they...most of them have no fathers or mothers, or else...and they have to go live in foreign countries or live in a forest...and they even have to change their clothes and pretend they're men. They're very much thrown on their own resources. That's what they learn. There are four or five that I admired most – but I knew I wouldn't be like them. So I chose one of the lesser ones, one of the easier ones –

MRS. MOWBREY. I remember. I remember. That play. I can't remember its name – but that Kate had an awful temper. Mr. Lubbock, has our Kate got an awful temper? *(KATY stiffens.)*

LUBBOCK. No, indeed, Mrs. Mowbrey.

KATY. No, I wish I did. I think people with a temper are lucky.

MRS. MOWBREY. Lucky! How could you wish a thing like that.

KATY. When things seem all wrong to me, I do something worse than have a temper. I turn all cold and stormy inside. It's as though something were dead in me.

MRS. MOWBREY. I understand every word of that. Katy, dear, we will be good friends. – Now surely there's some furniture I can lend you, some household appointments?

KATY. *(quietly)* Thank you very much, Aunt Julia. But, of course, we mean to live very simply. And we won't be seeing anyone for the first year or two. – Will we John?

LUBBOCK. *(floundering)* Just as you wish, Katy…

MRS. MOWBREY. Oh, dear! That's so unwise! My dear children, you must come and see *me* – and my friends. I have so many friends who will be delighted to meet you: artists and writers and young men in politics – so valuable for Mr. Lubbock's work. And the dear rector of my church, Mr. Jenkins.

KATY. All that's for John to decide, of course.

(**KATY** *turns inquiringly toward him, as does* **MRS. MOWBREY.**)

LUBBOCK. *(belatedly he stammers)* Oh, we…won't be seeing too many people…

MRS. MOWBREY. There's Judge Whittaker's son for example. You'll laugh till the tears run down your cheeks. *(with confidential emphasis to* **KATY***)* Judge Whittaker can do anything in New York – *anything* you ask him…Old friend of mine. *(to* **LUBBOCK,** *rising)* People with influence like that – you must know them. *(to* **KATY***)* And then I want to take you shopping, dear. Stores where they know me. They practically *give* me the things. Great Heavens, I haven't had to pay the marked [price] for anything, for years. Friends, friends everywhere. – Now I'm going to leave you two alone together. I know you have a world of things to talk about.

(**KATY** *rises*)

If you want some more tea, just ring and ask Marget for it.

KATY. *(always quietly)* Aunt Julia, I can see John perfectly well in my own home. I came to call on you.

MRS. MOWBREY. *(moving to the door)* What a sweet thing to say. – No, no. I know young people in love; don't say I don't. And beginning today I want you to think of this house as your second home. Besides, I have a present for you and I must go and get it. *(She indicates a ring on her finger.)* A very pretty thing, indeed.

KATY. *(following* **MRS. MOWBREY** *toward the door; with a touch of firmer protest)* But, Aunt Julia! –

MRS. MOWBREY. Ten minutes! I'll give you ten minutes!

(She goes out. **KATY** *turns and with lowered eyes goes slowly to her chair. She sits and covers her face with her hands.)*

KATY. *(as though to herself)* I can't understand it…What a dreadful, dreadful person.

LUBBOCK. *(uncomfortable)* Come now, Katy. It's not as bad as all that…Of course, she's a little…odd; but I imagine she's been through a lot of…trouble of some sort.

(**KATY** *looks at him a moment and then says with great directness.)*

KATY. What has she done, John? *(He doesn't answer.)* It must be something serious. Mother won't talk about her *one minute!* – Tell me! What is it?

LUBBOCK. Well…uh…she may have made some wrong step…early in life. Something like that.

KATY. *(after weighing this thoughtfully)* No. My mother would have forgiven that…It must be something much worse.

LUBBOCK. Whatever it was it's behind her. It's in the past.

KATY. *(shakes her head; she gives a shudder)* It's there – *now. (always very sincerely, this as though to herself)* I don't even know the names of things. Except what I've read about. In books. *(brief pause) (as with an effort to say such an awful thing)* Was she a…usurer?

LUBBOCK. What's that? – Oh, a usurer. *(with too loud a laugh)* NO, no – she wasn't that!

KATY. Was she a perjurer?

LUBBOCK. Katy, where do you get these old expressions? I don't know, but I guess she wasn't that.

KATY. *(gravely pursuing her thought) Was* she…that other kind of bad person. That word that's in the Bible and in Shakespeare… *(this takes solemn courage)* …that begins with "double-you"…with "double-you aitch" – ?

(This takes a minute to dawn on **LUBBOCK.** *He reacts violently; with as little comic effect as possible.)*

LUBBOCK. Katy!! How can you say such a thing.

KATY. I don't know how to pronounce it.

LUBBOCK. Do stop this! Put this all out of your head, *please.*

KATY. But she's my own aunt. I must have some idea to go by. Mother won't say a word. She just bursts into tears and leaves the room.

LUBBOCK. Please, Katy. – For Heaven's sake, change the subject.

KATY. I don't want to know anything that it's *unsuitable* for me to know. But I don't want to live with people hiding things from me. I don't think ignorance helps anybody. I can see perfectly well that you know the answer: Was Aunt Julia that thing that beings with "double-you"?

LUBBOCK. I'm not going to answer you, Katy. This conversation is unsuitable. Very unsuitable.

KATY. *(who has kept her eyes on him; calmly)* Then she *was.*

LUBBOCK. No – I didn't say that. Anyway, how would I know a thing like that? – Probably, she was just connected with such things – at a distance.

KATY. How do you mean?

LUBBOCK. She wasn't in it herself…She just – sort of stood by…I'm not going to stay here another moment. Where's that woman put my hat?

KATY. I see…She arranged them. That's in Shakespeare, too. She was a bawd.

LUBBOCK. Katy!

KATY. It's in the Bible, too: she was a... *(She pronounces the "aitch.")* whoremonger. *(She rises.)*

LUBBOCK. *(fiercely)* Stop this right now. How can you say such ugly words?

KATY. Are there any others that aren't ugly? – Anyway, now I know. *(She quickly moves up toward the entrance.)*

LUBBOCK. Where are you going?

KATY. *(from the steps)* You don't want me to stay, do you?

LUBBOCK. Think a moment, Katy. Stop and think.

KATY. Think what?

LUBBOCK. Well...this Bible you're quoting from...should have taught you to be charitable about people's mistakes. About Mary Magdalene and all that.

KATY. *(turning in deep thought)* Yes, it should, shouldn't it? – But Mary Magdalene wasn't the second thing; she was the first. *(She returns to her chair and sits, her eyes on the floor. Again as though to herself.)* I don't know anything about anything. *(She suddenly looks at him and says with accusing directness.)* And you're not helping me. Tell me what I should think. Are you going to be like this always?...When I ask questions?...

LUBBOCK. *(urgently)* No, Katy. I promise you. I'll answer anything you ask me!

KATY. When?

LUBBOCK. When we're married. – But not here! Not now! – Today, anyway, put all this out of your head.

KATY. *(reluctantly acquiescent, rises again)* When we're married. That's like what Mother's always saying: "When you're older; when you're older." *(turning to him with decision)* But if she *is* those things – those things that Shakespeare said –

LUBBOCK. Don't say them!

KATY. Promise me that you'll never see her again.

LUBBOCK. Now, K-a-a-ty! She's a client. In business we can't stop to take any notice of our client's morals...

KATY. In business they don't? I mean: thieves and criminals? Don't men meet that kind of people all the time?

LUBBOCK. *(putting his hands over his ears)* Questions! Questions! You're going to drive me crazy.

KATY. *(looking around the room, musingly)* And all this money came from...that! *(her eyes return to him)* And when she asks us to come here to dinner?

LUBBOCK. Of *course*, we don't have to come often. But she's a lonely woman who's trying to put the mistakes of her life behind her. Be kind, Katy. Be charitable!

KATY. *(weighs this, then says simply)* Have you ever seen her before?

LUBBOCK. Mrs. Mowbrey? *(loud laugh of protest)* Of *course* not.

(KATY goes to the hall. From the top step she turns and says with great quiet but final significance.)

KATY. And you want me to invite her to the wedding?

(LUBBOCK cannot answer. His jaw is caught rigid. KATY returns into the room, drawing a ring off her finger.)

All I know is what I read in Shakespeare and the Bible. That's all I have to go by, John. Nobody else helps. You don't help me. I'm giving you back your ring.

(She puts the ring on the taboret and goes quickly, with lowered head, out of the house. The front door is heard closing. LUBBOCK stands rigid. Slowly he goes to the taboret and takes up the ring. MRS. MOWBREY appears at the hall indignant.)

MRS. MOWBREY. Who went out the front door? Was that Katy?

(He puts down the ring on the taboret.)

LUBBOCK. Yes, Mrs. Mowbrey. She went home.

MRS. MOWBREY. *(coming in)* Without saying good-bye to me! Her own aunt! Well – there's a badly brought up girl! *(sitting down)* What did she say?

LUBBOCK. She left no message.

MRS. MOWBREY. I'm ashamed of her, Mr. Lubbock. I never heard of such behavior. The idea! *(seeing the ring)* What's this? What's this ring?

LUBBOCK. She left it. It's her engagement ring.

MRS. MOWBREY. She broke her engagement? *(rising)* Mr. Lubbock, listen to me! You can call yourself a very lucky man. One look at her, and I could see she wasn't the right girl for you. – Left without saying one word of good-bye! I don't know what's become of the girls these days. A niece of mine – behaving like that. *(giving him the ring and wagging her finger in his face)* Now you must put that in a safe place – and you'll find the real right girl for you. They aren't all dead yet. You're going to find some splendid girl and I'm going to make a second home for you here. We're going to have fun. *You only live once,* as the Good Book says.

LUBBOCK. *You* did this! Look! *(holding the ring toward her)* She's gone. – You with your conniving and sticking your nose into other people's business. WHY the hell did you have to put your goddamned nose into my affairs?

MRS. MOWBREY. I have never allowed profanity to be used in my presence.

LUBBOCK. Well, you'll hear it now. You – with your sentimental whining about wanting friends. *You'll* never have any friends. You don't deserve to have any friends. God, have you wrecked your chances today! – While you were wrecking mine.

(She has descended coolly into the room. **LUBBOCK** *passes her toward the hall)*

You can sit here alone for ever and ever, as far as I care. Where'd that girl put my hat?

MRS. MOWBREY. Yes, Mr. Lubbock, you go and you stay away. You have just shown yourself to be the biggest fool I ever saw. It wasn't I that lost you that girl; it was yourself. And you deserve to lose her.

LUBBOCK. How do you know what happened?

MRS. MOWBREY. I will ring and Marget will get your hat. *(She pulls a bell rope. The waiting.)* Katy is my niece. Every inch my niece. She put you to the test and you were... *(vituperatively) Shown up. Shown up.* Oh, you men! On your high saddles.

LUBBOCK. I tried to save you, anyway.

MRS. MOWBREY. I never saw anyone so stupid.

(enter **MARGET***)*

MARGET. Yes, Mrs. Mowbrey.

MRS. MOWBREY. Mr. Lubbock's been looking for his hat, Marget.

MARGET. Yes, ma'am.

*(***MARGET*** disappears and returns with a straw hat. ***LUBBOCK*** takes it. ***MARGET*** disappears. ***LUBBOCK*** lingers at the top of the stairs.)*

LUBBOCK. Well – out with it. What should I have done?

MRS. MOWBREY. In the first place you should have lied, of course. Strong and loud and clear. A girl like that is not ready to learn what she wants to know. And at this stage it's not your business or mine to tell her.

LUBBOCK. She said she left me because I wasn't any help to her. Is lying any help?

MRS. MOWBREY. Of course it is. I suppose you think you were trying to tell her the truth? Young man, you're not old enough to tell the truth and it doesn't look as though you ever will be. In the first place, you should have lied, firmly, cleanly. THEN, you should have shown her that you *were* her friend. Katy did just right. Katy left you standing here, because she saw that you never would be her friend – that you haven't the faintest idea what it is to be a friend. What took place here took place in my own life. It's taking place all the time. Mr. Lubbock, people don't like to be –

*(***LUBBOCK*** rises, crosses the room and says aggressively and a little brutally:)*

LUBBOCK. Mrs. Mowbrey, this has all been very interesting; and you've played your various cards very neatly and all that, but I want to know why you really asked me to come and see you today.

MRS. MOWBREY. *(also getting tougher)* I am coming to that. *(she pauses)* Do you prefer to stand?

LUBBOCK. *(shortly)* Yes, I do.

MRS. MOWBREY. There's one event in your life – in our lives – that I'd like you to explain to me. One night, at The Palace – it was in the spring of – you lost your head, or rather you lost control of yourself. You broke every bottle in my bar. You did like that with your arm. *(Her arm makes wide sweeping gestures, from right to left and left to right.)* You terrorized everyone. You didn't strike anyone, but the flying glass could have blinded my girls. You weren't drunk. What happened? What made you do that?

LUBBOCK. *(furious, but coldly contained)* I paid for it, didn't I?

MRS. MOWBREY. Oh, Mr. Lubbock. Don't talk like a child. You and I know that there are a great many things that can't be paid for. – Was it something that Dolores said to you – or that I said to you? *(pause)* Or did that friend of yours – what was his name? Jack Wallace or Wallop? – did he hurt your feelings? No, it couldn't be that; because you didn't strike *him.* The only thing you struck was a lot of bottles and *you weren't drunk.*

(She waits in silence; finally he says in barely controlled impatience.)

LUBBOCK. What of it? What of it? I lost my temper, that's all.

MRS. MOWBREY. I can understand your losing your temper at *people*, Mr. Lubbock – we all do; but I can't understand your losing your temper at *things.*

LUBBOCK. What are you trying to get at, ma'am? Out with it. Are you trying to tell me that you think I'm not fit to be the husband of your niece?

MRS. MOWBREY. No, indeed. I think you're just the right husband for her; and the more I talk to you, the more I think you're just the right lawyer for me.

(**LUBBOCK** *is stunned by this sudden shift in* **MRS. MOWBREY**'s *attitude.*)

Now, do you know what I have out in the sun porch? Do you? *(He shakes his head in confusion.)* A bottle of champagne. And do you know what Lena is looking at in the kitchen? Two great big steaks.

LUBBOCK. *(slowly recovering himself)* I don't really like champagne, Mrs. Mowbrey; but would you happen to have any bourbon in the house?

MRS. MOWBREY. Bourbon! Have I bourbon? After six o'clock that's all I touch. *(guiding him to the door)* And if you're a good boy I'll show you the list of my investments. There are one or two I'm worried about. Really worried.

[(She pauses at the top step; he beside her. She puts her hand on his arm.)]

We all have disappointments in life, John – everyone of us – but remember Shakespeare said –

[(She smiles and taps him significantly on the chest with her jeweled forefinger.)]

you know –

[(She laughs and exits. He stands a moment, uncertain, then notices the straw hat still in his hand. He descends into the room, and gazes thoughtfully about. Then he places his straw hat on the taboret, turns and quickly exits in the direction **MRS. MOWBREY** *has taken. The Lights fade.)]*

End of Play

A NOTE ON THE TEXT

The author's manuscript of *In Shakespeare and the Bible* existed in three nearly completed drafts, the latest of which had a number of rewrites, additions and corrections toward a fourth draft. Pages and sections of the earlier drafts, which were lined through or crossed-out, have been examined but have not played a significant part in assembling this version of the play. Wilder's habit of throwing out what he emphatically rejected *("The writer's best friend is his wastepaper basket," is a motto he often articulated)*, but keeping around what he might refer to again and use again provided a richly marked road map to the play printed here.

Wilder leaves us wondering whether John will succumb to the strong impulse to grab success at any cost. For this reason I added stage directions [*in brackets*] at the end to give John a moment to collect his thoughts, wonder what the right path is, and then, at least for the moment, to cave in.

F. J. O'Neil
April, 1997

SIX

SOMEONE FROM ASSISI

(Lust)

CHARACTERS

PICA, a twelve-year-old girl
MONA LUCREZIA, a crazy woman, forty
MOTHER CLARA, a sister at Saint Damian's, thirty-one
FATHER FRANCIS, a visiting priest, forty

SETTING

Poor Sisters Convent at Saint Damian's near Assisi.

(The kitchen-garden behind the convent. A number of low benches surround the playing area. The actors' entrance at the back represents a door into the convent; it is framed by a trellis covered with vines. Opposite, the aisle through the audience represents a path to the village street. A young girl, PICA, *twelve, barefoot and wearing a simple smock, comes running out of the convent; she stares down the aisle through the audience and starts to shout in anger and grief.)*

PICA. No! No! Old Crazy – go home! You mustn't come here today. Go home! Go HOME!! We have someone especially important coming and you mustn't be here! Go home! You'll spoil everything!

*(*MONA LUCRETIA, *looking much older than her forty years, comes lurching through the audience to the stage. She is crazy. Her black, gray and white hair is uncombed. She carries a large soiled shawl. She mumbles to herself as she advances.)*

MONA. Don't make such a noise, child. I must think what I'm going to say when he comes. Now, *you* go away. I must think.

PICA. No, *you* go away. – Oh, this is terrible!

*(*PICA *turns and rushes into the convent, calling:)*

Mother Clara! Mother Clara!

MONA. *(shouting)* It's I who have someone important coming – not you. And... *(worriedly)* I must be ready. It's so hard to be ready. I must put gold on my hair... and perfumes, more perfumes. He'll have elephants and...camels.

*(*MOTHER CLARA, *thirty-one, enters and stands at the convent door looking thoughtfully at* MONA LUCRETIA. PICA *passes her and comes toward the center of the stage.)*

PICA. Mother, she mustn't be here today when *he* comes. Tell old Thomas to drive her away. She'll sing and make a noise and spoil everything. – Old Crazy, *go home!* Mother Clara, we would die of shame, if *he* heard the things she says.

CLARA. *(quietly, her gaze on* **MONA***)* Be quiet, Pica. – Mona, do you know me? – What is her name, Pica?

PICA. I don't know. I've forgotten.

CLARA. Go and ask Old Thomas what her name is. I don't want you to call her Old Crazy. – Has she a home to go to?

PICA. Oh, Mother – she is very rich. But her family drives her out of the house all day.

*(**MONA** has seated herself on one of the benches, her elbows on her knees. She is staring at the ground.)*

CLARA. Go and find out what her name is.

*(**PICA** runs into the convent.)*

Mona, do you know me?…Mona, do you know me? I am Mother Clara of the Poor Sisters at Saint Damian's. Do you know me?…What is your name?

MONA. *(rising; impressively)* I am who I am. – *He* is coming today. You know I am the Queen of…

CLARA. What?…Who is coming?

MONA. The King of…

CLARA. Yes. What king?

MONA. *(becoming confused)* The King of Solomon. To see me. I must be ready. He is coming…from France. And…

CLARA. From France?!!

MONA. Of course, from France. I must have presents to give him. And…He will have lions. And…

CLARA. Yes. You must be ready, Mona.

*(In order to induce **MONA** to leave the garden, **CLARA** crosses the stage and starts walking backward through the audience.)*

CLARA. Come. You must go to your home and make yourself ready. Look!…Just look! You must comb your hair
beautifully. And you must *wash your face*! – Who is it
you say is coming?

MONA. *(following her; angrily)* I *told* you – the King of
Solomon…Of France. That is: French France. I didn't
love him – *no!*; but he loved me. But now he has
become a great person and he sends me all these mes-
sages.

*(Stopping at the edge of the stage, She looks at the floor in
a troubled way; softly:)*

Did I tell you the truth? Did I love him? Did I? – Oh,
he wrote such songs for me. Songs and songs.

CLARA. Come, Mona. I think you should rest, too.

MONA. *(confidentially)* If I walk slowly he will not see that I
am lame. One of the boys in the street kicked me.

CLARA. Kicked…!! Yes, walk slowly. Like a queen. No, no,
stand up straight, Mona – like a queen. You can do it.
Come. What will you say when you see the king?

MONA. I shall say…*(standing straight)* Oh, King of Solomon,
I shall say: Change the world!

CLARA. *(astonished)* You will say that?

MONA. They throw stones at me. They kick me. Everywhere
people hate people. My daughters – with brooms –
they drive me away. I can't go home; I can only go
home when the sun goes down. And I shall say oh,
King, change the hearts of the world.

CLARA. *(returns to the stage; as* **MONA** *passes her on the way to
the village)* That is a very good thing to say. You won't
forget it?

MONA. *(loudly)* The world is *bad*.

CLARA. Yes.

MONA. Nobody is kind anymore.

CLARA. You tell your daughters that Mother Clara of Saint
Damian's says that they are to let you into the house;
and you will wash your face and your hair, won't you?
And God bless you, dear Mona, and make you wise…
wise and beautiful…for your friend.

(**MONA** *has almost disappeared. From the convent sounds of joyous cries and laughter.* **PICA** *comes running out like an arrow.*)

PICA. *(shrilly)* He has come, Mother Clara. Father Francis is here!

(She flies back into the convent.)

MONA. *(returning a few steps)* What did you say?…Wise?

CLARA. Yes…and beautiful. Good-bye, Mona. Remember. Good-bye.

MONA. *(mumbling)* Wise…and beautiful…

(She goes out.)

(**FRANCIS** *appears at the convent door. He is forty, browned by the weather, almost blind, and with very few teeth. Also he is very happy.* **CLARA**, *joyously, and as lightly as a young girl, runs to the center of the stage and falls on her knees.*)

CLARA. Bless me, Father.

FRANCIS. *(kneels, facing her)* God bless you, dearest Sister, with all His love. – And now you bless me, Sister.

CLARA. *(lowered eyes, laughing protest)* Father!

FRANCIS. Say after me God bless you, Brother Francis, and God forgive you that load of sins with which you have offended Him.

CLARA. God bless you, Brother Francis, with all His love.

FRANCIS. And…

CLARA. *(rippling laughter of protest)* I cannot say that, Father.

FRANCIS. I order you by your holy obedience.

CLARA. …And God forgive you that load of sins Father! – with which you have offended Him. – There!

FRANCIS. Yes.

(They both stay on their knees a moment, looking at one another, radiantly. **FRANCIS** *rises first and says with a touch of earnest injunction.)*

I want you to say that prayer…that *whole* prayer…for me, every day.

CLARA. I will, Father. – Now sit in the sun. The meal will be ready very soon.

FRANCIS. *(sitting)* And how is my little plant?

CLARA. *(again soft running laughter)* Your little plant is very well, Father.

FRANCIS. Let me see…was it ten years ago we cut off your beautiful hair and found you a bridegroom?

CLARA. Ten years ago next month.

FRANCIS. Yes…Never, Sister Clara, have I seen a more beautiful wedding…

CLARA. *(blushing with pleasure)* Father!

FRANCIS. *(softly)* …Except, of course, my own.

CLARA. Oh, yes – *yours.* We know all about that – to the Lady Poverty.

FRANCIS. The Lady Poverty.

CLARA. Yes. – And how are *you*, dear Father?

FRANCIS. Well…Well…

CLARA. And your eyes?

FRANCIS. Oh, Sister…I can see the path. I can see the brothers and sisters. I can see the Crucified on the wall.

CLARA. Oh, then, I'm so happy. I'd heard that you had some difficulty.

FRANCIS. *(emphatically)* Oh, yes, I can *see. (confidentially)* Maybe I'm a little bit blind; but…I *hear* so well. I *hear* so much better.

CLARA. Do you?

FRANCIS. Everything talks all the time. The trees. And the water. And the stones.

CLARA. *(holding her breath)* What, Father?

FRANCIS. The stones. The rocks. Now, when I go up there to pray, I must say to them: "Be quiet."

CLARA. "Be quiet."

FRANCIS. "Be quiet for a while." And they are quiet.

CLARA. Yes, Father.

(There is a moment while she digests this; then she begins again with animation.)

My sisters are so happy that you have come. Sister Agnes has made something for you. Now promise that you will eat all of it. It will break her heart if you don't.

FRANCIS. All?

CLARA. *(laughing)* Oh, it is very little. We have learned that.

FRANCIS. All? My stomach has grown so small… *(making a ring with his thumb and forefinger)* …That is enough.

CLARA. We understand. But this time there is a touch – a touch of saffron.

FRANCIS. Saffron!!

CLARA. The Count sent it to us from the castle, especially for you. He remembered that you liked it…*before…*

FRANCIS. Before? Before when?

CLARA. Well…Father…before…Before you entered the religious life.

FRANCIS. *(agitated)* Before!!? When I was the most sinful of men! No, no, Sister Clara! Go quickly and tell Sister Agnes – no saffron! No saffron.

CLARA. *(calling sharply and clapping her hands)* Pica! Pica!

*(**PICA** enters at once.)*

PICA. Yes, Mother.

CLARA. Tell Sister Agnes *no* saffron in Father's dish. And do not stand by the door.

PICA. Yes, Mother.

*(During this interchange, **MONA** has returned, mumbling, through the audience.)*

MONA. They throw stones at me. They kick me. Hmm. But when the king comes they will learn who I am. Hmm. They will sing another song.

CLARA. *(her eyes again thoughtfully on* **MONA***, who has seated herself on one of the benches)* She has lost her wits…She comes of a prosperous family, but they send her out of the house all day. I think the children torment her. She likes to come and sit here, rain or shine. – Father – she thinks she is the Queen of Sheba! And that King Solomon is coming to visit her!

FRANCIS. *(delighted)* She thinks she is…! How rich she is. How happy she must be!

CLARA. *(pointing to her own forehead)* Yes – but she is touched.

FRANCIS. Touched?…Oh, touched. – Is she able to receive the blessed sacrament?

CLARA. No. I think not. They tell me that in church she cries out and says unsuitable things. No, she is not allowed in the church.

FRANCIS. What is her name?

CLARA. Everyone here seems to have forgotten it. They simply call her Old Crazy. We call her Mona.

FRANCIS. *(taking a few steps toward* **MONA***)* Mona!…Yes, your king is coming.

MONA. *(violently)* Go away from me! I know all about your nasty filthy wicked ways!

CLARA. *(authoritatively)* Now, Mona, you must be quiet or we will send you away – with a broom, too. You know our Thomas. Our Thomas knows how to make you move.

FRANCIS. *(quiets* **CLARA** *with a gesture; his eyes on* **MONA** *in reflection)* Who can measure the suffering – the waste – in the world? And every being born into the world – except One – has added to it. You and I have made it more and more.

(He turns to **CLARA** *and adds with eager face:)*

Let us go to the church now and fall on our knees. Let us ask forgiveness.

CLARA. Father, we shall go to the church later. Now you have come here to take the noon meal with my dear sisters.

FRANCIS. *(with a sigh, as of a pleasure postponed)* Yes...yes.

CLARA. *(resuming the animated tone)* You received my letter? We can't give thanks enough! More and more are coming all the time. Sometimes I'm at my wit's end to find room and food for all these girls and women who are coming to join us. Oh, but I won't trouble you with *those* things – beds and food. We always find a way.

FRANCIS. Yes. Yes. No one would believe how we always find more beds and food.

CLARA. And their happiness! From morning to night. – You will hear them sing. They have been learning some new music to sing to you.

FRANCIS. *(rising, stuttering with eagerness)* Sister C-C-Clara, let us go into the chapel and thank God.

CLARA. We will. We will. But now, dear Father, just for a moment, let us sit in the sun and rest ourselves.

FRANCIS. *(again resigned)* ...Yes...Very well.

CLARA. Father, there is something I've long wanted to ask you. Can we talk for a moment of childish things? – Father, you will eat the noonday meal at our table today? You will?

FRANCIS. Sister! Sister! Can't I have it out here? *Where* I eat it is of no importance. I shall see the sisters later when I preach to them.

CLARA. Father, you hurt them.

FRANCIS. Hurt them?! I hurt them?

CLARA. They cannot understand it. You let Brother Avisio and Brother Juniper eat with us.

FRANCIS. Yes...yes...

CLARA. But you have never sat down with us at our table... Why is that? *(lowering her voice)* My sisters are beginning to believe that you think that women are of a *lower order* in God's love.

FRANCIS. Sister Clara!!

CLARA. They have heard that you share your meal with... wolves and birds, but never with *them*. – Can the Father Francis whom we love – this once – sit down with us women?

FRANCIS. *(agitated slightly but compliant)* Yes…oh, yes…I will.

CLARA. *(urgently)* It is so important, Father. I work among these good women and girls. They have left everything. They have God in Heaven but they have very little on earth. *(He nods repeatedly.* Thank you! Now there's another childish thing I want to ask you. Brother Avisio told me a short time ago that you were christened John. Is that true?

FRANCIS. Yes. Yes. John.

CLARA. You chose the name Francis?

FRANCIS. My friends gave it to me. But that's long ago.

MONA. *(from under the hood of her shawl, as though brooding to herself)* Francis the Frenchman…They all called him that. That's what I called him, too.

(after **FRANCIS** *and* **CLARA** *have looked at* **MONA** *a moment)*

FRANCIS. Long ago – when I was a young man. Before I found something better, I was never tired of hearing all those songs and stories that came down from France…about knights in armor who went about the world killing dragons and tyrants. A growing boy must have something to admire – to make his heart swell. I talked about those stories to everyone I knew. I dressed myself in foreign dress. I made songs, too – many of them. And…but…

CLARA. Why do you stop, Father?

FRANCIS. And I heard that each of these knights had a lady. *(He looks at her with pain and appeal.)* I looked everywhere. I…I…looked everywhere.

CLARA. Do not talk of it, if it distresses you.

FRANCIS. *(low and urgently)* …May God forgive me that load of sin with which I offended him!

CLARA. Yes.

FRANCIS. I went through a troubled time… *(Suddenly he looks at her happily.)* And then I found my lady.

CLARA. *(laughing)* Yes, we know, Father.

FRANCIS. Poverty! And I married her!

CLARA. Yes.

FRANCIS. And ever since, I go about the world singing her praises.

CLARA. Yes.

FRANCIS. *(eagerly)* Before I knew her I was a coward. Yes. I was afraid of everything: of going into the forests at night; I was afraid of hunger and of cold. I was afraid to knock at the doors of nobles and great people. But *now* – with *her* beside me – I go everywhere. I do not trouble when I go into the Pope's presence, even. I am not afraid when twenty new brothers arrive at our house: where shall I put them? How shall I feed them? She shows me.

(CLARA nods in complete agreement.)

But how can one say how beautiful she is! And .... and *(lowering his voice)* how severe. Sometimes I almost offend her. And then I know that her eyes are *turned away* from me!... *(suddenly raising his hands)* No saffron! No saffron! – But most of the time we live together in great happiness.

(He crosses the stage, groping in his memory for an old song.)

...That song...that old song I wrote for her:

When in the darkness of the night
I see no lantern and no star,
My lady's eyes will bring me light.
When in pathless woods I stray
My feet have stumbled in despair
My lady's eyes will show the way.

MONA. When prison chains do fetter me –

FRANCIS. *(a loud cry of recognition)* Mona Lucrezia!!

MONA. *(harshly)* Shame on you! To sing that song in the ears of a holy woman! *That* is Mother Clara of Saint Damian's. Cover your ears, Mother Clara. *(advancing on FRANCIS)* What do you know of Francis the

Frenchman? *I* know him. He wrote that song for me.

When prison chains do fetter me
And it is written I must die
My lady's eyes will set me free.

Yes, we all knew that he searched for his lady. We all knew that – the mayor's wife and Ninina Dono...and I...

FRANCIS. Mona Lucrezia. *(trembling, to* **CLARA***)* Leave me alone with her.

MONA. Mother Clara, they say that he goes all over the world now; that he sees the Pope and says good morning, good morning; that he's gone to Palestine to convert the Grand Turk himself –

CLARA. Do not be long, Father. The meal is almost ready.

(She hurries out.)

MONA. *(calling after her)* He said my body was of marble and snow – no, he said that my body was of fire and snow.

(She starts leaving the stage through the audience.)

He'll convert the Grand Turk. The Devil will help him. He converted the mayor's wife and me – the Devil helping him.

*(***FRANCIS***, shaken and speechless, stands looking after her.* ***PICA*** *has entered stealthily from the convent.* ***FRANCIS*** *appears not to hear her.)*

PICA. Father Francis, we did everything we could to prevent that crazy woman from coming here today. Mother Clara says that you are going to sit at table with the sisters – for the first time. You must sit quite still during the reading because Sister John of the Nails is going to draw a picture of you that we can have on the wall. When people draw you, you have to sit very still, because when you move, they can't see what to draw – *(sounds of shouting from the street)*

MONA. *(offstage)* Go away from me! Peter, put down that stone! Aiiiiiiee!

PICA. Oh, Father Francis! She's coming back again. They've been throwing stones at her.

(She goes down the aisle.)

Don't...come...back. We'll beat you!

FRANCIS. Come here and be quiet!

(MONA lurches back, shouting toward the street. One side of her face is covered with blood. She is struck again and sinks on one knee at the edge of the stage.)

MONA. Pigs – all of you. Lock your mothers up and there'll be no more of you.

FRANCIS. Come and sit down here, Mona Lucrezia.

MONA. *(to FRANCIS)* Don't strike me – you! Go away from me.

FRANCIS. *(authoritatively to PICA)* Get a bowl of water and a clean cloth. Put some leaves and stems of the hazel into it. And be quick.

(PICA stands gaping.)

Be quick! Be quick!

(PICA runs off.)

MONA. *(harshly to FRANCIS)* You kicked me!

FRANCIS. No, Mona Lucrezia.

MONA. You did.

FRANCIS. Come over here and sit down. You are among friends now.

MONA. *(sitting down)* There are no friends. I don't want any friends. I had some.

(She stares at FRANCIS, somberly.)

Who are you? What's your name?

FRANCIS. I was christened John.

MONA. John! – Do you know who John was?

FRANCIS. *(in a small voice)* Yes.

MONA. You stand there – idle as a log – and *do* nothing. If all the men in the world named John would join themselves together and be worthy of their name, the world would not be like that.

FRANCIS. Don't put your hand on your wound, Lucrezia. We'll wash it in a moment.

MONA. *(harshly)* Don't talk to me! *(silence) (then broodingly to herself)* The king will look for me. "Where is my queen?" I'll hide where he can't find me. – And I had something to tell him.

(CLARA enters swiftly with water and a cloth. She kneels before MONA.)

CLARA. Hold your face up, Mona Lucrezia.

MONA. Don't touch me! You are a holy woman. I will do it myself. Or let that log do it – that worthless John.

(As though overcoming a powerful repulsion, FRANCIS applies the wet cloth to MONA's forehead.)

MONA. *(striking him)* That hurts.

FRANCIS. Yes, it will hurt for a minute. Sit quiet. Sit quiet.

MONA. *(with a sob, but submitting)* That hurts.

(At a signal from FRANCIS, CLARA leaves.)

FRANCIS. There, that's better. Now your hands...

MONA. *(with closed eyes)* They wash the dead. They washed us when we were born.

(silence)

FRANCIS. Now your face again.

MONA. No! Don't touch me again. I don't like to be touched.

(She takes the cloth.)

(grumbling as though to herself) On an important day like this!...And you one of those great good-for-nothing monks, filling your big belly with meals at other people's tables. *(directly at him, fiercely)* God must weep!

FRANCIS. Yes.

MONA. Francis the Frenchman became a monk. I knew him. I never said to him what I should have said. It was clear in my mind, like writing on the wall; but I never said it. Whatever Francis the Frenchman wanted to do, oh, he did it. His will was like...! It was that that made us break our vows. I had never deceived my husband. I told him I was afraid of God. What do you suppose he said? I told him I was afraid of losing God's love. *(She stares at him.)* He said: all love is one!

FRANCIS. No-o!

MONA. He said that he would make me the lady of his life and that he would do anything that I ordered him to do...I should have ordered him to do...that though that was like writing on the wall. Even then, though I was a girl, I knew that the world was a valley without rain...a city without food. I knew...I felt...he could... *(She becomes confused.)*

FRANCIS. *(low)* What would you have said, Lucrezia?

MONA. *(rising)* I shall be your lady. And I command you: OWN NOTHING. No one will listen to you, if you have a roof over your head. No one will listen to you if you know where you will eat tomorrow. It is fear that has driven love out of the world and only a man without fear can bring it back. *(She glares at him a moment, then sinks back on the bench.)* But I never said it!

FRANCIS. Lucrezia, do you know me? I am Francis.

MONA. *(without interest)* No, you are some other Francis. I am going now.

FRANCIS. *(calling)* Pica! Pica!

MONA. *(starting to the town)* I'm tired...but I'm afraid of the butcher's dog...and the mayor's –

FRANCIS. Pica!

(PICA rushes in.)

I am taking Mona Lucrezia to her home. *(He indicates with his eyes.)* I will need you to show me the way.

PICA. Father Francis, the sisters are ready to sit down at the table. You will break their hearts.

MONA. *(starting)* I had a stick. The boys are always taking away my stick. *(stopping)* Someone was coming to town today...

PICA. *(spitefully)* Yes! Father Francis himself. And you've spoiled everything!

FRANCIS. *(to* **PICA***)* Hsh! – I cannot see the path. Give me your hand.

MONA. *(turning)* Those dogs – the butcher's Rufus. Brother John, haven't you got a stick?

PICA. *(giggling)* She doesn't even know that dogs don't bite Father Francis!

MONA. *(stopping and peering at* **FRANCIS***)* Haven't you got a stick?

FRANCIS. No, Mona Lucrezia. I have nothing.

(They go out.)

End of Play

SEVEN

CEMENT HANDS

(Avarice)

CHARACTERS

EDWARD BLAKE, a lawyer, fifty
PAUL, a waiter, fifty-five
DIANA COLVIN, Blake's niece, twenty-one
ROGER OSTERMAN, Diana's fiancé, twenty-seven

SETTING

Corner in the public rooms of a distinguished New York hotel.

(A screen has been placed at the back [that is, at the actors' entrance] to shut this corner off from the hotel guests. A table in the center of the stage with a large RESERVED sign on it. Various chairs. At the end of the stage farthest from the entrance is a low bench; above it we are to assume some large windows looking onto Fifth Avenue. Enter **EDWARD BLAKE**, *a lawyer, fifty. He is followed by* **PAUL**, *a waiter, fifty-five.)*

BLAKE. *(rubbing his hands)* Paul, we have work to do.

PAUL. Yes, Mr. Blake.

BLAKE. There will be three for tea. I arranged with Mr. Gruber that this corner would be screened off for us; and I specially asked that you would wait on us. As I say, we have some work to do. *(smilingly giving him an envelope)* There's a hundred dollars, Paul, for whatever strain you may be put to.

PAUL. Thank you, sir. – Did you say "strain," Mr. Blake?

BLAKE. I'm going to ask you to do some rather strange things. Are you a good actor, Paul?

PAUL. Well – I often tell the young waiters that our work is pretty much an actor's job.

BLAKE. I'm sure you're a very good one. Now the guests today are my niece, Diana Colvin. – You know Miss Colvin, don't you?

PAUL. *(with pleasure)* Oh, yes, Mr. Blake. Everyone knows Miss Colvin.

BLAKE. And her fiancé – that's a secret still – Mr. Osterman?

PAUL. Which Mr. Osterman, sir?

BLAKE. Roger – Roger Osterman. You know him?

PAUL. Oh, yes, sir.

BLAKE. Now it's not clear which of us is host. But it's clear to *me* which of us is host. Roger Osterman has invited us to tea. He will pay the bill.

PAUL. Yes, sir.

BLAKE. There may be some difficulty about it – some distress; some squirming; some maneuvering – protesting. But he will pay the bill.

(a slight pause while he looks hard and quizzically at **PAUL,** *who returns his gaze with knowing raised eyebrows)*

Now at about 5:20 you're going to bring Mr. Osterman a registered letter. The messenger will be waiting in the hall for Mr. Osterman's signature. Roger Osterman will ask to borrow half a dollar of me. I won't have half a dollar. He will then turn and ask to borrow half a dollar of you. And you won't hear him.

PAUL. I beg your pardon, sir?

BLAKE. He'll ask to borrow half a dollar of you, but you won't hear him. You'll be sneezing or something. Your face will be buried in your handkerchief. Have you a cold, Paul?

PAUL. No, sir. We're not allowed to serve when we have colds.

BLAKE. Well, you're growing deaf. It's too bad. But...you... *won't...hear* him.

PAUL. *(worriedly)* Yes, sir.

BLAKE. You'll say, *(raising his voice)* "Yes, Mr. Osterman, I'll get some hot tea, at once." This appeal to you for money may happen several times.

PAUL. *(abashed)* Very well, Mr. Blake, if you wish it.

BLAKE. Now, Paul, I'm telling you why I'm doing this. You're an intelligent man and an old friend. My niece is going to marry Roger Osterman. I'm delighted that my niece is going to marry him. He's a very nice fellow and what else is there about him, Paul?

PAUL. Why, sir – it is understood that he is very rich.

BLAKE. Exactly. But the Ostermans are not only fine people and very rich people – they have oddities about them, too, haven't they? – A certain oddity?

(BLAKE *slowly executes the following pantomime: he puts his hands into his trouser pockets and brings them out, open, empty and "frozen".*)

PAUL. *(reluctantly)* I know what you mean, sir.

BLAKE. Have you a daughter, Paul, or a niece?

PAUL. Yes, sir. I have two daughters and three nieces.

BLAKE. Then you know: we older men have a responsibility to these girls. I have to show my niece what her fiancé is like. I have to show her this odd thing – this one little unfortunate thing about the Ostermans.

PAUL. I see, Mr. Blake.

BLAKE. I'm not only her uncle; I'm her guardian; and her lawyer. I'm all she's got. And I must show her – here she comes now – and for that I need your help.

(Enter **DIANA COLVIN**, *twenty-one, in furs. The finest girl in the world.*)

DIANA. Here you are, Uncle Edward. – Good afternoon, Paul.

PAUL. Good afternoon, Miss Colvin.

BLAKE. Will you wait for tea, Diana?

DIANA. *(crossing the stage to the bench)* Yes.

(**PAUL** *goes out.*)

BLAKE. Aren't you going to kiss me?

DIANA. No!! I'm furious at you. I'm so furious I could cry. You've humiliated me. I'm so ashamed I don't know what to do. Uncle Edward, how could you do such a thing?

BLAKE. *(calmly)* What, dear?

DIANA. I've just heard that –

(She rises and strides about, groping for a handkerchief in her bag.)

– you're asking the Osterman family how much allow- ance Roger will give me when we're married. And you're making some sort of difficulty about it. Uncle Edward! The twentieth century! And as though I were some poor little goose- girl he'd discovered in the country. Oh, I could die. I swear to you, I could die.

BLAKE. *(still calmly)* Sit down, Diana.

(Silence. She walks about, dabs her eyes and finally sits down.)

Diana, I'm not an idiot. I don't do things like this by whim and fancy.

DIANA. Perfectly absurd. Why, all those silly society colum- nists keep telling their readers every morning that I'm one of the richest girls in the country. Is it true?

(He shrugs.)

I'll never need a cent of the Ostermans' money. I'll never take a cent, not a cent.

BLAKE. What?

DIANA. I won't have to.

BLAKE. What kind of marriage is that?

(He rises. She looks at him a little intimidated.)

Well, you'll be making an enormous mistake and it will cost you a lot of suffering.

DIANA. What do you mean?

BLAKE. Marriage is a wonderful thing, Diana. But it's rela- tively new. Twelve, maybe fifteen thousand years old. It brings with it some ancient precivilization elements. Hence, difficult to manage. It's still trying to under- stand itself.

DIANA. *(shifting in her seat, groaning)* Really, Uncle Edward!

BLAKE. It hangs on a delicate balance between things of earth and things of heaven.

DIANA. Oh, Lord, how long?

BLAKE. Until a hundred years ago a wife *had* no money of her own. All of it, if she had any, became her husband's. Think that over a minute. Billions and billions of marriages where the wife had not one cent that she didn't have to *ask* for. You see: it's important to us men, us males, us husbands that we supply material things to our wives. I'm sorry to say it but we like to think that we own you. First we dazzle you with our strength, then we hit you over the head and drag you into our cave. We buy you. We dress you. We feed you. We put jewels on you. We take you to the opera. I warn you now – most seriously – don't you start thinking that you want to be independent of your husband as a provider. You may be as rich as all hell, Diana, but you've got to give Roger the impression every day that you thank him – thank him humbly, that you aren't in the gutter.

DIANA. *(short pause; curtly)* I don't believe you.

BLAKE. Especially Roger. *(leaning forward; emphatic whisper)* You are marrying into a very strange tribe.

(They gaze into one another's eyes.)

Roger is the finest young man in the world. I'm very happy that you're going to marry him. I think that you will long be happy – but you'll only be happy if you know beforehand exactly what you're getting into.

DIANA. What *are* you talking about?

(She rises and crosses the stage.)

I want some tea.

BLAKE. No, we don't have tea until he comes. *He* is giving us tea. Please sit down. What am I talking about? Diana, you've been out with Roger to lunch and dinner many times, haven't you? You've gotten in and out of taxis with him. You've arrived at railroad stations and had porters carry your bags, haven't you?

DIANA. Yes.

BLAKE. Have you ever noticed anything odd about his behavior in such cases?

DIANA. What do you mean?

(He gazes levelly into her eyes. She begins to blush slightly. Silence.)

BLAKE. Then you have?

DIANA. *(uncandidly)* What do you mean?

BLAKE. Say it!

(pause)

DIANA. *(suddenly)* I love him.

BLAKE. I know. But say what's on your mind.

DIANA. It's a little fault.

BLAKE. How little?

DIANA. I can gradually correct him of it.

BLAKE. That's what his mother thought when she married his father…After you leave a restaurant do you go back and leave a dollar or two for the waiter, when Roger's not looking? Do you hear taxi drivers shouting indecencies after him as he walks away? Have you seen him waste time and energy to avoid a very small expenditure?

DIANA. *(rising, with her handbag and gloves, as though about to leave)* I don't want to talk about this any more. It's tiresome; and more than that it's in bad taste. Who was it but *you* who taught me never to talk about money, never to mention money. And now we're talking about money in the grubbiest way of all – about *tipping.* And you've been talking to the Osterman family about an allowance for me. I feel soiled. I'm going for a walk. I'll come back in twenty minutes.

BLAKE. Good. That's the way you should feel. But there's one more thing you ought to know. Paul will help us.

(He goes to the entrance at the back, apparently catches **PAUL***'s eye, and returns.)*

DIANA. You're not going to drag Paul into this?

BLAKE. Who better? – Now if *you* sit at ease, it will put *him* at ease.

(*Enter* **PAUL.**)

PAUL. Were you ready to order tea, Mr. Blake?

BLAKE. No, we're waiting for Mr. Osterman. You haven't seen him, have you?

PAUL. No, I haven't.

BLAKE. Paul, I was talking with Miss Colvin about that little matter you and I were discussing. You gave me permission to ask you a few questions about the professional life in the hotel here.

PAUL. If I can be of any help, sir.

BLAKE. The whole staff of waiters is accustomed to a certain lack of…generosity on the part of the Osterman family. Is that true?

PAUL. (*deprecatingly*) It doesn't matter, Mr. Blake. We know that they give such large sums to the public in general…

BLAKE. Is this true of any other families?

PAUL. Well…uh…there's the Wilbrahams.

(**BLAKE** *nods.*)

And the Farringtons. That is, Mr. Wentworth and Mr. Conrad Farrington. With Mr. Ludovic Farrington it's the other way 'round.

BLAKE. Oh, so every now and then these families produce a regular spendthrift?

PAUL. Yes, sir.

BLAKE. I see. Now, have the waiters a sort of nickname for these less generous types?

PAUL. (*reluctantly*) Oh…the younger waiters…I wouldn't like to repeat it.

BLAKE. You know how serious I am about this. I wish you would, Paul.

PAUL. Well…they call them "cement hands."

DIANA. (*appalled*) WHAT?

BLAKE. *(clearly)* Cement hands. – What you mean is that they can give away thousands and millions but they cannot put their fingers into their pockets for…a quarter or a dime? And, Paul, is it true that in many cases the wives of the Ostermans and Wilbrahams and Farringtons return to the table after a dinner or supper and leave a little something – to correct the injustice?

PAUL. Yes, Mr. Blake. – Mrs….but I won't mention any names…sometimes sends me something in an envelope the next day.

BLAKE. Yes.

PAUL. Perhaps I should tell you a detail. In these last years, the gentlemen merely *sign* the waiter's check. And they add a present for the waiters in writing.

BLAKE. *That* they can do. Well?

PAUL. Pretty well. What they cannot do –

BLAKE. – is to put their hands in their pockets. Thank you. And have you noticed that one of these hosts…as the moment approaches to…

(He puts his hands gropingly in his pockets.)

…he becomes uncomfortable in his chair…his forehead gets moist?…

PAUL. Yes, sir.

BLAKE. He is unable to continue conversation with his friends? Some of them even start to quarrel with you?

PAUL. I'm sorry to say so.

BLAKE. *(shakes* PAUL*'s hand)* Thank you for helping me, Paul.

PAUL. Thank you, sir.

(PAUL goes out. DIANA sits crushed, her eyes on the ground. Then she speaks earnestly.)

DIANA. Why is it, Uncle Edward? Explain it to me! How can such a wonderful and generous young man be so mean in little things?

BLAKE. Your future mother-in-law was my wife's best friend. Katherine Osterman has given her husband four children. She runs two big houses – a staff of twenty at least. Yet every expenditure she makes is on account it goes through her husband's office – sign for everything – write checks for everything. You would not believe the extent to which she has no money of her own – in her own hand. Her husband adores her. He can't be absent from her for a day. He would give her hundreds of thousands in her hands but she *must ask for it.* He wants that picture that everything comes from him. Why, she has to go to the most childish subterfuges to get a little cash – she buys dresses and returns them, so as to have a hundred dollars in bills. She doesn't want to do anything underhand, but she wants to do something personal – small and friendly and personal. She can give a million to blind children, but she can't give a hundred to her maid's daughter.

(**DIANA,** *weeping, blows her nose.*)

Now you say you have your own money. Yes, but I want to be sure that you have an allowance *from Roger* that you don't have to account to him for. Money to be human with – not as housekeeper or as a beautifully dressed Osterman or as an important philanthropist but as an imaginative human being; and I want that money to come from your husband. It will puzzle him and bewilder him and distress him. But maybe he will come to understand the principle of the thing.

DIANA. *(miserably)* How do you explain it, Uncle Edward?

BLAKE. I don't know. I want you to study it right here today. Is it a sickness?

DIANA. *(shocked)* Uncle Edward!

BLAKE. Is it a defect in character?

DIANA. Roger has no faults.

BLAKE. Whatever it is, it's deep – deep in the irrational. For Roger it's as hard to part with twenty-five cents as it is for some people to climb to the top of a skyscraper, or to eat frogs, or to be shut up with a cat. Whatever it is – it proceeds from a *fear*, and whatever it is, it represents an incorrect relation to –

DIANA. To what?

BLAKE. *(groping)* To…

(**PAUL** *appears at the entrance.*)

PAUL. Mr. Osterman has just come into the hall, Mr. Blake.

BLAKE. Thank you, Paul.

(**PAUL** *goes out.*)

DIANA. Incorrect relation to what?

BLAKE. To material things – and to circumstance, to life – to everything.

(*Enter* **ROGER OSTERMAN**, *twenty-seven, in a rush. The finest young fellow in the world.*)

ROGER. Diana! Joy and angel of my life.

(*He kisses her.*)

Uncle Edward. – Ten minutes past five. I've got to make a phone call. To Mother. I'll be back in a minute. Mother and I are setting up a fund. I'll tell you all about it. Uncle Edward, what are you feeding us?

BLAKE. We haven't ordered yet. We were waiting for our host.

ROGER. *(all this quickly)* Am I your host? Very well. You've forgotten that you invited us to tea. Didn't he, Diana?

BLAKE. You distinctly said –

ROGER. *You* distinctly said – really, Diana, we can't let him run away from his responsibilities like that. Uncle Edward, we accept with pleasure your kind invitation –

BLAKE. You called me and told me to convey your invitation to Diana. Diana, thank Roger for his kind invitation.

DIANA. *(rising, with a touch of exasperation)* Gentlemen, gentlemen! Do be quiet. The fact is *I* planned this party and you're both my guests. So do your telephoning, Roger, and hurry back.

ROGER. You're an angel, Diana. Tea with rum in it, Uncle Edward.

DIANA. Come here, you poor, poor boy.

(She looks gravely into his eyes and gives him a kiss.)

ROGER. *(laughing)* Why am I a poor, poor boy?

DIANA. Well, you are.

(She gives him a light push and he goes out laughing.)

BLAKE. We must act quickly now. I've arranged for some things to happen during this hour. You're going to spill some tea on your dress – no, some chocolate from a chocolate éclair.

DIANA. What?!

BLAKE. And you'll have to go to the ladies' room to clean it up. And you're going to need fifty cents. Open your purse. Give me all the change you have – under a five dollar bill.

DIANA. Why?

BLAKE. Because you'll have to borrow the fifty-cent piece from *him.* – Give me your change.

DIANA. Uncle Edward, you're a devil.

(But she opens her handbag and purse.)

BLAKE. *(counting under his breath)* Three quarters. Fifty-cent piece. Dimes. No dollar bills.

DIANA. *(crossing the room, in distress)* Uncle, I don't believe in putting people to tests.

BLAKE. Simply a demonstration –

DIANA. I don't need a demonstration. I suffer enough as it is.

BLAKE. But have you forgotten: we're trying to learn something. Is it a sickness or is it a –

DIANA. Don't say it!

BLAKE. And I want you to notice something else: every subject that comes up in conversation… *(He starts laughing.)*

DIANA. *(suspicious and annoyed)* What?

BLAKE. To call your attention to it, I'll *(He drops his purse.)* drop something. Every subject that comes up in the conversation will have some sort of connection with money.

DIANA. *(angrily drops her handbag)* But that's all you and I have been talking about – until I'm about to go crazy.

BLAKE. Yes…yes, it's contagious.

DIANA. *(with weight)* Uncle Edward, are you trying to break up my engagement?

BLAKE. *(with equal sincerity, but quietly)* No! I'm trying to ratify it…to *save* it.

DIANA. How?

BLAKE. *(emphatic whisper)* With…understanding.

(Enter PAUL.)

Oh, there you are, Paul. Tea for three and a decanter of rum. And a chocolate éclair for Miss Colvin.

DIANA. But I hate chocolate éclairs!

*(**BLAKE** looks at her rebukingly.)*

Oh, all right.

BLAKE. And, Paul, when we've finished tea, you'll place the check beside Mr. Osterman.

*(**DIANA** purposefully drops her lipstick.)*

PAUL. *(picking up the lipstick)* Yes, sir.

DIANA. Thank you, Paul.

*(**PAUL** goes out. **DIANA** leans toward **BLAKE** and says confidentially:)*

Now you must play fair. If you cheat, I'll stop the whole thing.

*(Enter **ROGER**.)*

ROGER. All is settled. It's really very exciting. Mother and I setting up a fund where there's a particular particular need.

DIANA. What is it, Roger?

ROGER. *(laughs; then)* Guess where Mother and I are going tomorrow?

DIANA. Where?

ROGER. To the poorhouse!

(BLAKE pushes and drops the ashtray from the table.)

DIANA. *(covering her ears)* Uncle Edward, do be careful!

ROGER. In fact, we're going to three. Mother's already been to thirty – in England and France and Austria – I've been to ten. We're doing something about them. We're making them attractive. Lots of people come to the ends of their lives without pensions, without social security. We're taking the curse off destitution.

BLAKE. And you're taking the curse off superfluity.

(DIANA looks at BLAKE hard and drops her gloves.)

ROGER. We're beginning in a small way. Mother's giving two million and Uncle Henry and I are each giving one. We're not building new homes yet – we're improving the conditions of those that are there. Everywhere we go we ask a thousand questions of superintendents, and of the old men and women…And do you know what these elderly people want most?

(He looks at them expectantly.)

DIANA. *(dropping a shoe)* Money.

ROGER. *(admiringly)* How did you know?!

(DIANA shrugs her shoulders.)

You see, in a sense, they have everything – shelter, clothes, food, companionship. We've scarcely found one who wishes to leave the institution. But they all want the one thing for which there is no provision.

(PAUL enters with a tray – tea; rum; éclair; the service check, which he places on the table beside ROGER; and a letter.)

PAUL. A letter has come for you, Mr. Osterman, by special messenger. Will you sign for it, Mr. Osterman?

ROGER. For me? But no one else knows that I'm here.

BLAKE. By special messenger, Paul?

PAUL. Yes, Mr. Blake.

BLAKE. And is the messenger waiting? *(intimately)* Roger… the messenger's waiting in the hall…

ROGER. What?

BLAKE. Fifty cents…for the messenger.

ROGER. *(a study)* But I don't think this is for me.

(He looks at it.)

DIANA. *(taking it from him)* "Roger Osterman, Georgian Room, etc." Yes, I think it's for you.

(ROGER makes some vague gestures toward his pockets.)

ROGER. Uncle Edward…lend me a quarter, will you?

BLAKE. *(slowly searching his pockets)* A quarter…twenty-five cents…Haven't got it.

ROGER. Paul, give the boy a quarter, will you?

PAUL. *(deaf as a post)* Hot water? Yes, Mr. Osterman –

ROGER. *(loud)* No…a QUARTER, Paul…give the boy a quarter…

PAUL. It's right here, Mr. Osterman.

ROGER. *(has torn the letter open; to BLAKE)* It's from you. You say you'll be here. Well, if the messenger boy is from your own office, you can give him a quarter.

BLAKE. *(smiting his forehead; gives quarter to PAUL)* That's right…Paul…I'll see you…

ROGER. *(dabbing his forehead with his handkerchief)* My, it's hot in here.

DIANA. Roger – you were saying that these old people wanted money. They have everything provided, but they still want money.

ROGER. Yes, I suppose it's to give presents to their nephews and nieces...to one another...They have everything except that...

(He starts laughing; then leans forward confidentially and says:) You know, I think one of the reasons Mother became so interested in all this was...

(Then he stops, laughs again, and says:) Anyway, she's interested.

DIANA. What were you going to say?

ROGER. *(reluctantly)* Well...she's always had the same kind of trouble.

(The other two stare at him.)

Do you know that Mother once pawned a diamond ring?

BLAKE. Your mother went to a pawnshop?

ROGER. No. She sent her maid. Even today she doesn't know that I know. – I was at boarding school, and I'd begun a collection of autographs. More than anything in the world I wanted for my birthday a certain letter of Abraham Lincoln that had come on the market. I couldn't sleep nights I wanted it so bad. But Father thought it was unsuitable that a fifteen year old should get so worked up about a thing like that. – So Mother pawned her ring.

*(**DIANA** rises and crosses the room. She is flushed and serious.)*

DIANA. I don't think we should be talking about such things – but – let me ask one thing, Roger. Your mother has always had a great deal of money of her own?

ROGER. *(laughing)* Yes. But, of course, Father keeps it for her. More than that he's doubled and tripled it.

BLAKE. Of course. It passes through his hands.

ROGER. Yes.

BLAKE. *(looking at* **DIANA***)* He sees all the checks. Like the old people in the poorhouse, your mother has everything except money?

ROGER. *(laughing)* Exactly! – The other thing the old people are interested in is food –

DIANA. *(looking down at her dress)* Oh! I've spilled some of that tea and rum on my dress. I must go to the ladies' room and have the spot taken out. Uncle Edward, lend me half a dollar for the attendant.

BLAKE. *(ransacking his pockets)* Half a dollar! Half a dollar! – I told you I hadn't a cent.

ROGER. In institutions – like prisons and poorhouses – you never have any choice –

DIANA. Roger, lend me half a dollar.

ROGER. *(taking out his purse, as he talks)* That was the awful part about prep school – all the food –

(He hands **DIANA** *a ten-dollar bill and goes on talking.)*

– was, so to speak, assigned to you. You never had the least voice in what it would be.

DIANA. But I don't want ten dollars. I want fifty cents.

ROGER. What for?

DIANA. To give the attendant in the ladies' room.

ROGER. Fifty cents? *(rising and inspecting her dress)* I don't see any stain. *(to* **BLAKE***)* Borrow it from Paul.

BLAKE. Paul's deaf. Roger, put your hands in your pockets and see if you haven't got fifty cents.

DIANA. *(almost hysterically)* It's all right. The stain's gone away. Forget it, please. Forgive me. I've made a lot of fuss about nothing.

ROGER. *(again touching his forehead with his handkerchief)* Awfully warm in here. We ought to have gone to the club. These places are getting to be regular traps. Why did we come here?

DIANA. What do you mean – traps?

ROGER. You're interrupted all the time – these tiresome demands on you. I love to give, but I don't like to be held up *(gesture of putting a revolver to someone's head)* held up every minute. *(a touch of too much excitement)* I'd like to give everything I've got. I don't care how I live; but I don't like to be forced to give anything. It's not *my* fault that I have money.

DIANA. You're right, Roger.

(She sees **PAUL**'s *service check on the table. She flicks it with her finger and it falls on the floor as near the center of the stage as possible.)*

I don't think of a tip as an expression of thanks. It's just a transaction – a mechanical business convention. Take our waiter, Paul. My thanks is in my smile, so to speak. The money on the table has nothing to do with it.

ROGER. Well, whatever it is, it's a mess.

BLAKE. Once upon a time there was a very poor shepherd. It was in Romania, I think.

DIANA. Uncle!

BLAKE. Every morning this shepherd led his sheep out to a field where there was a great big oak tree.

DIANA. Really, Uncle!

BLAKE. And one day – under that oak tree – he found a large gold piece. The next day he found another. For weeks, for months, for years – every day – he found another gold piece. He bought more sheep. He bought beautiful embroidered shirts.

*(***DIANA** *is suddenly overcome with uncontrollable hysterical laughing. She crosses the room, her handkerchief to her mouth, and sits on the bench by the windows.* **BLAKE** *waits a moment until she has controlled herself.)*

No one else in the village seemed to be finding any gold pieces.

*(***DIANA** *sputters a moment.* **BLAKE** *lowers his voice mysteriously.)*

BLAKE. The shepherd's problem was – *Where do they come from?* And *why* are they given to *him?* Are they, maybe... supernatural?

ROGER. *(sharply)* What?

(BLAKE points to the ceiling.)

I don't understand a word of this. Uncle Edward, do get on with it. I've never been able to understand these...allegories.

BLAKE. But why to *him?* Was he more intelligent – or more virtuous than the other young men? *(pause)* Now when you find a gold piece every morning, you get used to it. You get to need them. And you are constantly haunted by the fear that the gold pieces will no longer appear under the oak tree. What – oh, what can he do to insure that those blessed gold pieces will continue to arrive every morning?

(BLAKE's voice turns slightly calculatedly superstitious; he half closes his eyes, shrewdly. His blade-like hand descries an either-or decision or bargain.)

Obviously, he'd better *give*. In return, so to speak. He gave his town a fine hospital. He gave a beautiful altar to the church.

(He changes his voice to the simple and direct.)

Of course, he gave. But this shepherd was a fine human being, and it was the other question that troubled him most-frightened him, I mean: Why have I been *chosen?*

DIANA. *(sober; her eyes on the floor)* I see that he became frightened.

ROGER. *(looking at DIANA, in surprise – laughing)* You understand what he's talking about?

DIANA. Frightened, because...if the gold pieces stopped coming, he'd not only be poor...he'd be much more than poor. He'd be exposed. He'd be the man who was formerly fortunate, formerly – what did you say? – intelligent, formerly virtuous and –

BLAKE. *(pointing to the ceiling)* Formerly favored, loved.

DIANA. Far worse than poor.

BLAKE. So he was in the terrible situation of having to GIVE all the time and of having to SAVE all the time.

DIANA. Yes...Yes. – Roger, I have to go. *(She rises.)* Now, who's going to pay the bill? – Roger, you do it, just to show that you like to.

ROGER. *(with charming spontaneity)* Of course, I will. Where is it?

DIANA. *(pointing)* Right there on the floor.

ROGER. *(picking it up)* I'll sign for it. – Where's Paul? There he is!

DIANA. *(putting on lipstick and watching him in her mirror)* Surely, it's not large enough to sign for. There's something small about signing for a three or four dollar charge.

ROGER. *(looking from one to the other)* I don't think so.

BLAKE. Diana's right.

ROGER. *(taking a ten-dollar bill from his purse and laying it on the bill)* Diana, some day you must explain to me slowly what Uncle Edward's been talking about.

(Enter PAUL. ROGER indicates the money with his head. PAUL makes change quickly.)

Paul, we're leaving. *(to DIANA)* And you must make your Uncle Edward promise not to get tied up in any long rambling stories he can't get out of.

DIANA. *(to PAUL)* Thank you, Paul.

BLAKE. Thank you, Paul.

ROGER. Thank you, very much, Paul.

PAUL. *(as he goes out, leaving the bill and change on the table)* You're very welcome.

ROGER. *(While he talks, is feverishly figuring out his change.)* Because I must be very stupid...I can't...

(His hand among the coins of change, he turns and says:) Because I must say there are lots of better things to talk about than what we've been...

(He stops while he studies the change before him.)

ROGER. In fact, in our family we make it a rule never to talk about money at all… *(pause)* I don't think you realize, Diana, that my life is enough of a hell as it is: the only way I can cope with it is to never talk about it…what am I doing here?…

DIANA. *(going toward him; soothingly)* What's the matter, dear? Just leave him a quarter.

ROGER. *(His face lighting up.)* Would that be all right?

(She nods.)

Diana, you're an angel. *(triumphantly)* I'm going to leave him fifty cents, just to show him I love you.

DIANA. No. I'm not an angel. I'm a very human being. I'll need to be fed. And clothed. And –

ROGER. *(bewitched; kissing her gravely)* I'll see you have every-thing.

DIANA. I can look forward to everything?

ROGER. Yes.

DIANA. Like those old ladies in the poorhouse, I can look forward to –

ROGER. My giving you everything.

(DIANA hurries out ever so lightly, blowing her nose. PAUL appears at the door. BLAKE and ROGER go out. PAUL, alone, picks up the tip. No expression on his face. DIANA appears quickly.)

DIANA. I dropped a glove.

(She drops a dollar bill on the table.)

Goodbye, Paul.

PAUL. Goodbye, Miss Colvin.

(They go out.)

End of Play

Also by
Thornton Wilder...

The Alcestiad, or A Life in the Sun
The Beaux' Stratagem (with Ken Ludwig)
The Matchmaker
Our Town
The Skin of Our Teeth

Thornton Wilder One Act Series: The Ages of Man
Infancy
Childhood
Youth
Rivers Under the Earth

Thornton Wilder One Act Series: Wilder's Classic One Acts
The Long Christmas Dinner
Queens of France
Pullman Car Hiawatha
Love and How to Cure It
Such Things Only Happen in Books
The Happy Journey to Trenton and Camden

Please visit our website **samuelfrench.com** for complete
descriptions and licensing information.

OTHER TITLES AVAILABLE FROM SAMUEL FRENCH

THE MATCHMAKER

Thornton Wilder

Farce / 9m, 7f / Multiple Interior

A certain old merchant of Yonkers is so rich in 1800 that he decides to take a wife. He employs a matchmaker a woman who subsequently becomes involved with two of his menial clerks, assorted young and lovely ladies, and the headwaiter at an expensive restaurant where this swift farce runs headlong into a hilarious complications. After everyone gets straightened out romantically and has his heart's desire, the merchant finds himself affianced to the astute matchmaker herself. He who was so shrewd in business is putty in the hands of Dolly Levi. He is fooled by apprentices in a series of hilarious hide and seek scenes, and finally has all his bluster explode in his face.

"Loud, slap dash and uproarious…extraordinarily
original and funny."
– *The New York Times*

"Rolls along merrily and madly and the customers are convulsed."
– *New York Journal American*

"The lines of Wilder are so often brilliant, sage, and witty."
– *New York Daily News*

OTHER TITLES AVAILABLE FROM SAMUEL FRENCH

OUR TOWN

Thornton Wilder

Drama / 17m, 7f, extras / Bare Stage

Winner of the 1938 Pulitzer Prize for Drama

In an important publishing event, Samuel French, in cooperation with the Thornton Wilder estate is pleased to release the playwright's definitive version of *Our Town*. This edition of the play differs only slightly from previous acting editions, yet it presents *Our Town* as Thornton Wilder wished it to be performed. Described by Edward Albee as "…the greatest American play ever written," the story follows the small town of Grover's Corners through three acts: "Daily Life," "Love and Marriage," and "Death and Eternity." Narrated by a stage manager and performed with minimal props and sets, audiences follow the Webb and Gibbs families as their children fall in love, marry, and eventually—in one of the most famous scenes in American theatre—die. Thornton Wilder's final word on how he wanted his play performed is an invaluable addition to the American stage and to the libraries of theatre lovers internationally.

"While all of Wilder's work is intelligent, non-synthetic and often moving, as well as funny, it is *Our Town* that makes the difference. It is probably the finest play ever written by an American."
– *Edward Albee*

"Thornton Wilder's masterpiece…An immortal tale of small town morality [and]…a classic of soft spoken theater."
– *The New York Times*

"Beautiful and remarkable one of the sagest, warmest and most deeply human scripts to have come out of our theatre…
A spiritual experience."
– *The New York Post*

SAMUEL FRENCH STAFF

Nate Collins
President

Ken Dingledine
Director of Operations,
Vice President

Bruce Lazarus
Executive Director,
General Counsel

Rita Maté
Director of Finance

ACCOUNTING

Lori Thimsen | Director of Licensing Compliance
Nehal Kumar | Senior Accounting Associate
Helena Mezzina | Royalty Administration
Glenn Halcomb | Royalty Administration
Jessica Zheng | Accounts Receivable
Andy Lian | Accounts Payable
Charlie Sou | Accounting Associate
Joann Mannello | Orders Administrator

CUSTOMER SERVICE AND LICENSING

Brad Lohrenz | Director of Licensing Development
Laura Lindson | Licensing Services Manager
Kim Rogers | Theatrical Specialist
Matthew Akers | Theatrical Specialist
Ashley Byrne | Theatrical Specialist
Jennifer Carter | Theatrical Specialist
Annette Storckman | Theatrical Specialist
Dyan Flores | Theatrical Specialist
Sarah Weber | Theatrical Specialist
Nicholas Dawson | Theatrical Specialist
Andrew Clarke | Theatrical Specialist
David Kimple | Theatrical Specialist

EDITORIAL

Amy Rose Marsh | Literary Manager
Ben Coleman | Editorial Associate
Caitlin Bartow | Assistant to the Executive Director

MARKETING

Abbie Van Nostrand | Director of Corporate
    Communications
Ryan Pointer | Marketing Manager
Courtney Kochuba | Marketing Associate

PUBLICATIONS AND PRODUCT DEVELOPMENT

Joe Ferreira | Product Development Manager
David Geer | Publications Manager
Charlyn Brea | Publications Associate
Tyler Mullen | Publications Associate
Derek P. Hassler | Musical Products Coordinator
Zachary Orts | Musical Materials Coordinator

OPERATIONS

Casey McLain | Operations Supervisor
Elizabeth Minski | Office Coordinator, Reception
Coryn Carson | Office Coordinator, Reception

SAMUEL FRENCH BOOKSHOP (LOS ANGELES)

Joyce Mehess | Bookstore Manager
Cory DeLair | Bookstore Buyer
Jennifer Palumbo | Bookstore Order Dept. Manager
Sonya Wallace | Bookstore Associate
Tim Coultas | Bookstore Associate
Alfred Contreras | Shipping & Receiving

LONDON OFFICE

Felicity Barks | Rights & Contracts Associate
Steve Blacker | Bookshop Associate
David Bray | Customer Services Associate
Zena Choi | Professional Licensing Associate
Robert Cooke | Assistant Buyer
Stephanie Dawson | Amateur Licensing Associate
Simon Ellison | Retail Sales Manager
Jason Felix | Royalty Administration
Susan Griffiths | Amateur Licensing Associate
Robert Hamilton | Amateur Licensing Associate
Lucy Hume | Publications Manager
Nasir Khan | Management Accountant
Simon Magniti | Royalty Administration
Louise Mappley | Amateur Licensing Associate
James Nicolau | Despatch Associate
Martin Phillips | Librarian
Zubayed Rahman | Despatch Associate
Steve Sanderson | Royalty Administration Supervisor
Douglas Schatz | Acting Executive Director
Roger Sheppard | I.T. Manager
Panos Panayi | Company Accountant
Peter Smith | Amateur Licensing Associate
Garry Spratley | Customer Service Manager
David Webster | UK Operations Director

GET THE NAME OF YOUR CAST AND CREW IN PRINT WITH SPECIAL EDITIONS!

Special Editions are a unique, fun way to commemorate your production and RAISE MONEY.

The Samuel French Special Edition is a customized script personalized to *your* production. Your cast and crew list, photos from your production and special thanks will all appear in a Samuel French Acting Edition alongside the original text of the play.

These Special Editions are powerful fundraising tools that can be sold in your lobby or throughout your community in advance.

These books have autograph pages that make them perfect for year book memories, or gifts for relatives unable to attend the show. Family and friends will cherish this one of a kind souvenier.

Everyone will want a copy of these beautiful, personalized scripts!

ORDER YOUR COPIES TODAY!
E-MAIL SPECIALEDITIONS@SAMUELFRENCH.COM
OR CALL US AT 1-866-598-8449!